1

The Black Idol!

Doctor James Hartley carefully lighted his cigar and leaned back in one of the comfortable padded leather chairs with which the big smoke-room on board the s.s. *Megalia* was so plentifully provided.

'I'm glad to have an opportunity of meeting you again, Mallory,' he said, blowing out a cloud of smoke and watching it slowly disperse. 'It must be nearly three years since I saw your father.'

The good-looking, fair-haired young man seated opposite him smiled rather gravely.

'I hope you'll remedy that as soon as we get to England, Dr. Hartley,' he replied. 'Father would be tremendously glad to see you if you could spare the time to run down for a few days.'

'I will,' said the other. 'I've been promising myself a holiday for months,

1

and unless something very urgent turns up I shall take advantage of your invitation at the first possible moment.'

He looked critically at the thin, lined face in front of him. Jack Mallory was only twenty-five, but he looked older, and even the coating of bronze with which a tropical sun had stained his cheeks failed to conceal the pallor and ravages of ill-health.

'You look as if you could do with a holiday, too,' he remarked.

The other laughed a trifle harshly.

'I'm all right,' he said and shrugged his shoulders. 'A bit worn out, that's all. I'll admit that I shan't be sorry to find myself amidst the peaceful surroundings of the country again. It'll be rather a pleasant contrast after the interior of China.' He sighed and took out a cigarette case with a hand that trembled slightly.

Hartley watched him fumbling with a cigarette, and frowned. He had known Jack Mallory almost from boyhood; had seen him a cheery schoolboy racing light-heartedly about the wooded acres of his Sussex home, and as a scarcely less

THE MENACE OF LI-SIN

When Doctor James Hartley meets up with the son of an old friend, he discovers that young Jack Mallory is in fear of his life. Having stolen the sacred Black Idol from the Temple of Tsao-Sun in China, he is being followed by emissaries of the Temple priests. Mallory is advised by Hartley to return the idol, but then it's stolen, sparking a series of murders. Both their lives, and those of their families and friends, are in danger . . .

Books by Nigel Vane
in the Linford Mystery Library:

THE VEILS OF DEATH

NIGEL VANE

THE MENACE OF LI-SIN

Complete and Unabridged

LINFORD
Leicester

First published in Great Britain

First Linford Edition
published 2011

British Library CIP Data

Vane, Nigel.
    The menace of Li-Sin. - -
    (Linford mystery library)
    1. Religious articles- -China- -Fiction.
    2. Theft- -Fiction. 3. Suspense fiction.
    4. Large type books.
    I. Title II. Series
    823.9'12–dc22

    ISBN 978–1–44480–648–9

Published by
F. A. Thorpe (Publishing)
Anstey, Leicestershire

Set by Words & Graphics Ltd.
Anstey, Leicestershire
Printed and bound in Great Britain by
T. J. International Ltd., Padstow, Cornwall

This book is printed on acid-free paper

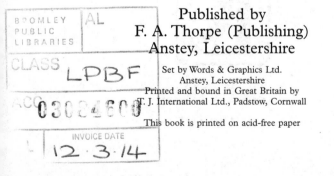

subdued youth just down from Cambridge; but there was something about him now that the doctor didn't understand. He seemed to have aged more than his years warranted, and there was a peculiar expression in his grey eyes that Hartley found difficult to place. He had noticed it on several occasions since Mallory had boarded the steamer at Singapore, and wondered inwardly at the cause. It was not fear nor suspicion but a combination of both — that quick sidelong glance that accompanied the approach of a stranger.

'Was your trip on business or merely pleasure?' he asked after a pause.

Jack's face clouded.

'Neither,' he answered shortly; and then, as though he was suddenly conscious of his abruptness: 'You certainly couldn't call it pleasure, and I doubt very much if business would be a strictly accurate description.' He looked quickly about him, assured himself that there was nobody else within earshot and lowering his voice almost to a whisper, he leaned towards the doctor: 'I think 'robbery' is

3

the only word suitable,' he said softly.

Dr. Hartley raised his eyebrows in startled surprise.

'My dear fellow,' he exclaimed, 'what on earth do you mean?'

'Well, that's what it amounted to,' replied Jack. 'I set out to get easy money.' He broke off and peered from side to side with that furtive sidelong glance that Hartley had noticed so many times before, then, apparently making up his mind, he said suddenly: 'Have you ever heard the story of the Temple of Tsao-Sun?'

Dr. Hartley started so violently that the cone of grey ash fell from the end of his cigar.

'The Temple of Tsao-Sun!' he repeated slowly and nodded. 'Yes, I have heard the legend. Why?'

'Because that's what brought me on this infernal trip,' answered Jack Mallory savagely. 'I came to find out if that legend was true, and it is. I've got the Black Idol in my cabin!'

The doctor stared at him, for the moment bereft of speech. It crossed his

4

mind that possibly his companion was joking, but a single glance at his set face convinced him that he was wrong.

'You've got the Black Idol — here!' he said. 'You mean you — ' He stopped, leaving the sentence unfinished.

'I mean I robbed the temple!' whispered Jack. 'I nearly lost my life, but I got away with what I went for.'

He crushed out the stub of his cigarette and lighted another. Puffing jerkily at the cylinder of tobacco, he continued:

'You know the story, Dr. Hartley. The Black Idol of Buddha is supposed to have stood in the Inner Temple of Tsao-Sun for thousands of years. It is quite a small statue of the Chinese god, barely three feet high, and wonderfully carved out of some hard wood that looks like marble. Generations ago there was a great rising amongst the people, an invasion from the north and robbers overran the whole place.' He moistened his dry lips with his tongue, but went on almost without a pause: 'According to the legend they sacked even the temples and the priests — those who had warning of their coming — stripped their robes and their temples of all the precious stones which they possessed and hid the most valuable within the hollow body of the Black Idol of Tsao-Sun!'

'Which is now in your possession,' murmured Dr. Hartley as the other paused.

'Yes,' Jack nodded.

'And the jewels?' asked the doctor. 'Did you find them inside according to the story?'

'I haven't been able to discover them so far,' answered his companion bitterly. 'There is an old manuscript in existence, I believe, which is supposed to have been handed down from one high priest to his successor, which describes how the idol is fashioned and contains directions for opening it, and they say that without these directions no man in the world could guess how to do it. I certainly have examined the thing carefully, but I can't see a sign of any possible aperture or break in the wood.'

He started and looked round uneasily as a steward passed on his way to another table.

'Surely a simple way of finding out whether it contains the jewels or not would be to break it up,' suggested Hartley, but Jack shook his head.

'The Chinese are a cautious race,' he replied, 'and they took precautions against that. The old legend states that if the idol is subjected to violence in any way, 'the earthquake follows.' In other words, the man who first told me the story and who, by the way, is the only European bar myself who has ever visited the temple, is convinced that when the jewels were stored away inside they were embedded in some kind of explosive.'

'H'm! Then, although you've got the idol, the prospect of finding the jewels seems rather remote,' commented Dr. Hartley. 'You appear to have taken a considerable risk for nothing.'

'And I am still running that risk — for nothing,' added Jack Mallory grimly.

The doctor's eyes narrowed suddenly.

'What exactly do you mean by that?' he asked sharply.

'I mean that ever since I got away from that infernal temple I've been followed,' said Jack. 'I couldn't tell you by whom because I've seen no one — that is, no one whom I could identify again — but I've been conscious of being — watched.'

'Are you sure of this?' said Hartley gravely. 'It's not just a figment of the imagination brought on by the knowledge that you are in possession of this idol?'

'I don't think so,' answered Jack. 'I've been aware of it ever since I got away from the temple.'

'Then if you take my advice,' said the doctor, 'you'll get rid of the Black Idol at the first opportunity.'

The other's jaw set stubbornly.

'Now I've got it I'm going to keep it,' he declared. 'I'm convinced that it contains the jewels, and somehow or other I'm going to find the way to get at them.'

Dr. Hartley looked at him steadily.

'I suppose you know,' he said after a pause, 'that if these people you believe to be following you are emissaries of the priests of the Temple of Tsao-Sun, you are carrying your life in your hands all the while that idol is in your possession?'

Jack nodded.

'Yes, I'm aware of that,' he answered. 'But I risked my life to get the thing, and I might as well risk a bit more to keep it.'

The doctor shrugged his shoulders.

'Well,' he said, 'if you like to be foolhardy, it's your look-out. Personally I think you're asking for trouble, and if you're not very careful you'll get it. It's dangerous to meddle with the religion of any race, and when you add the robbery of a considerable quantity of valuable jewels to the crime of violating the sacred precincts of a temple, it's suicidal.'

Jack lit another cigarette, but remained silent, and for a long time neither spoke, then Hartley, who had been staring at the table in front of him, thinking deeply, raised his eyes.

'What made you set out on this mad enterprise in the first place?' he asked. 'Just love of adventure?'

'No — want of money,' answered the other bitterly. 'You might not believe it, Dr. Hartley, but we're very poor. The estate is mortgaged up to the hilt, and if the interest, which falls due next month, isn't paid, the old place and everything it contains will be put up for sale, under the hammer. Father had tried every means in his power to raise the money, and when all else failed, I decided to have a go for the idol. I heard the story some years ago from a friend who lives in Pekin.'

'I had no idea things were as bad as that with you,' said the doctor sympathetically. 'But surely you could have raised money on the contents of Mallory Hall? The pictures and china alone must be worth a fortune.'

'They are,' said Jack, 'but unfortunately the estate is entailed — it has to pass intact to the next-of-kin — and therefore, legally we have no right to dispose of a single thing. Father had a long interview with the lawyers about it.'

'I see,' Hartley nodded. 'Of course in that case you could do nothing. But I must say I think you took a very risky way out, and since there appears, on your own showing, to be no means of finding out whether this idol really contains anything or not, you're not much better off than when you started.'

'That's perfectly true,' agreed Jack gloomily. 'I was hoping to be able to find the manuscript as well, which shows how to open the thing, and I would have done so if I'd had more time. You're rather good at puzzles, Dr. Hartley,' he added as a sudden thought struck him. 'Would you care to have a look at the idol and see if you can find any means of reaching the hollow space supposed to be inside?'

Dr. Hartley hesitated for a moment.

'I'd certainly like to see it, anyway,' he admitted presently, 'though I doubt very much whether I shall be any more successful in finding the key to the mystery than you have been. I know something about Chinese workmanship, and if the Black Idol was intended for a hiding-place for these jewels you can be sure that the job's been done thoroughly.'

'Come down to my cabin,' said Jack rising to his feet, and with the doctor at his elbow, strolled across to the door of the smoking-room.

A man who had been lounging on the deck outside the open porthole, under which they had been seated, smiled and crossed noiselessly to the iron deck-rail. When they passed a second later, he was gazing out across the moonlit sea, apparently absorbed in the view, but it only held his attention long enough for Jack and his companion to reach the former's cabin, for as they entered he turned and, lighting a cigarette, sauntered slowly in the same direction.

Jack switched on the light and closed the door and then, drawing the curtain over the porthole, he pulled out from under the bunk a long, narrow box of plain wood. It was fastened by a padlock, and, taking a key from his waistcoat pocket the young man unlocked it and opened the lid. Parting the straw with which the oblong box was filled, he lifted out a black object that gleamed in the light and stood it carefully on the wall-table beside the head of the bunk.

'Behold the Black Idol!' he said with a harsh laugh, and waved his hand towards it.

Dr. Hartley looked at the image, and caught his breath in admiration at the skilful hand of the carver. It was a little over three feet in height and represented a squatting figure reminiscent of Buddha. But whereas the Chinese god was usually pictured as a beneficent deity, this had the face of a devil! A malignant leer twisted the full, sensuous lips, and half-closed eyes peered out from under swollen, bloated lids with an expression of indescribable evil. It was as if the original artist had captured and entombed in that mass of carved wood every horrible desire and thought conceived by the mind of man since the world began.

'Nice little fellow, isn't he?' said Jack as Hartley continued to gaze spellbound at the image. 'The sort of thing to send one's maiden aunt, from whom one has expectations, on her seventy-fifth birthday!'

'It's a remarkable piece of work,' murmured Dr. Hartley interestedly, and going closer he examined the hideous idol with care. The wood, black as jet, was as hard and smooth as marble and shone as though with generations of polish. The doctor passed his long, slim sensitive fingers over the head and body, but he could not discover the slightest sign of a join anywhere or any possible aperture. If there was a means of reaching the interior of the image, it had been so cleverly concealed as to defy detection.

'I'm afraid the only way you will ever find whether this contains any jewels or not,' he said after a lengthy inspection, 'is to risk the chance of an explosion and break it up. So far as I can see, it's carved from a single block of wood, and appears solid.'

Jack nodded, surveying his possession with unfavourable eyes.

'I suppose that is the only way,' he agreed. 'I must say, though, that I'm doubtful if I could bring myself to do that even if there wasn't a risk of the thing blowing up. It would be almost an act of vandalism.'

'It would,' said Hartley. 'As a work of art the image is unique. One of the most wonderful pieces of carving I think I have ever seen.'

The dinner bugle sounded at that moment, and almost regretfully Jack

Mallory put the idol back in the shallow box, and carefully locking it, replaced it under the bunk. Shutting and locking his cabin door, he and Hartley made their way to the saloon. The second steward hurried forward to meet them, and showed them to their table. A girl who was seated at the captain's table smiled at Jack as they took their places, and he bowed in return.

'Remarkable things coincidences, when you come to think of it,' he said as Hartley picked up the menu. 'That girl is going to be a neighbour of ours. She and her uncle — the tall man sitting beside her — have bought Haslemere, which practically adjoins our estate. Funny we should both be on the same ship.'

'Who are they?' asked the doctor, giving his order and passing the menu over to his companion.

'He's pretty well known, I believe,' answered Jack. 'Professor Alington. I don't know what he professes, but I've heard the name before.'

'The author of *Ancient China*,' said Hartley, looking across the big saloon at

15

the white-haired, thin-faced man. 'He is very well known indeed. I've read his book but never seen the man before. He's an authority on everything Chinese.'

'Then I must get him to have a look at my idol,' said Jack with a laugh. 'He may be able to discover the secret.'

Dr. Hartley's face clouded, but he said nothing. One of those extraordinary intuitions that sometimes attacked his sensitive nature was making its presence felt. More than once during the course of his career, had he experienced that feeling — as of the abrupt lowering of the temperature — that prefaced danger, and he was experiencing it now strongly.

Somewhere lurked a menace, vague, intangible but potent, and it was connected with the Black Idol. He tried to put the feeling out of his mind, and turned the conversation into lighter channels, but it was there in spite of all his efforts, and remained a shadow at his elbow throughout the evening.

They strolled up and down the deck until eight bells was striking, and then, saying goodnight to the doctor, Jack made his way to his cabin, and began to undress, finding it hard to believe that in less than forty-eight hours he would be back home again amid the peaceful quiet of the country.

Getting into his bunk, he picked up a book and read for a quarter of an hour, and then, finding that his thoughts were wandering, and that he was incapable of fixing his mind on the printed page, he turned out the light, and lay for a long time in the darkness trying to woo the sleep that eluded him.

He must have succeeded in the end, though he couldn't have told the exact moment when consciousness left him, for he suddenly awoke with a chill sensation of fear and sat up in his berth. There was a squeak of a door-handle turning!

Before he had retired for the night, he had placed a small electric torch on the table within reach of his hand. Stealthily he stretched out and grasped it, and as the faint squeak was repeated, flashed a ray of light on a malignant yellow face peering in — the face of a Chinaman!

17

2

Murder!

In a second Jack Mallory was out of his bunk, but before his feet had touched the floor the door was jerked shut and the intruder had vanished.

The little alley-way outside was empty when he cautiously peered out, and when he reached the deck there was nobody in sight. He came back to his cabin and switching on the light, looked at his watch. It was three o'clock. He must have slept for longer than he had thought. His pulses were throbbing more with excitement than fear. There could be no doubt as to the reason for the Chinaman's presence. His conviction that he was being watched had received irrefutable proof, and there could be only one explanation — they were after the Black Idol! He went to the door and looked out. Where had the Chinaman come from and where had he gone? Most probably the steerage was an answer to both questions. He heard a sound in the corridor and saw the night steward coming towards him.

'Did you see anybody about just now?' he asked sharply stopping the man. 'A Chinaman?'

'A Chinaman?' repeated the astonished steward, and shook his head. 'No, sir, I haven't seen anybody.'

'Well, somebody tried to get into my cabin a few minutes ago,' said Jack, 'and I'll swear it was a Chinaman. Are there any Chinese on board in this ship?'

'There are one or two in the steerage, sir,' replied the steward. 'You say somebody tried to get into your cabin?' He went over and examined the catch on the door. 'There's nothing the matter with the lock,' he reported a few seconds later. 'Maybe you didn't close it, sir.'

There was something in his voice that suggested that he thought Jack had been either drunk or dreaming, and under the circumstances, the young man felt this belief was not unreasonable. He knew, however, that that malignant yellow face had been no figment of the imagination, and, when the night steward had passed on, he dressed and went on the promenade deck, where bare-footed deck-hands were washing down. The quartermaster in charge answered his questions in the negative.

'No, sir, I haven't seen anyone,' he said, and looked curiously after Jack as he mounted to the boat-deck.

The sky was growing grey and the morning air cold and keen, but there was not the sign of a soul about. The Chinaman had vanished completely. Without hesitation, Jack invaded that holy of holies, the bridge, and was promptly and courteously ordered down by the officer of the watch. That official had seen no one. Jack went back to the promenade deck and stood leaning over the rail, staring at the grey sea. Should he go and wake Dr. Hartley and tell him of his experience?

It seemed a selfish thing to do, but Jack had reached the state when he felt he had to tell someone. The grave uneasiness that had scarcely left him night or day, since his flight from the temple at Tsao-Sun, had reduced his nerves to shreds, and now he knew that that uneasiness was justified. He shivered slightly as he turned away from the rail, and the cause was not the keenness of the morning breeze. He had suddenly wondered what would have happened if he hadn't awakened at the precise moment when he did, and the thought was not a pleasant one.

Hartley's cabin was some distance from his own and he reached it without encountering anybody. Except for those on duty, the whole ship was sleeping.

'Who's there?' called the doctor's voice at once in answer to his tap, and Jack heard him give an exclamation as he replied. There was the creak of the bunk, the key snapped in the lock, and Hartley opened the door.

'What's the matter?' he said quickly, as Jack crossed the threshold, and the young man noticed that, although obviously just aroused from sleep, he was as alert as if it had been the middle of the afternoon.

As briefly as possible he related what

had happened, and the doctor listened gravely.

'A Chinaman, eh?' he muttered, when Jack had finished. 'H'm! Of course, he was after the Black Idol. I'm afraid you've stirred up a hornets' nest about your head. Candidly I think the best thing you could do would be to put that image in a conspicuous position and leave the cabin door open. If they get the thing back they'll probably leave you alone, but if you take it home with you — ' He shrugged his shoulders expressively.

'Your advice is undoubtedly good, Dr. Hartley,' said Jack, 'but' — he hesitated — 'I should hate to give it up without a struggle after all I went through to obtain possession of it.'

'You'll get all the struggle all right if you keep it,' retorted Hartley, 'and after all it's not really your property. To put it bluntly, you stole it, and you can scarcely blame the people to whom it really belongs for trying to get it back again.'

Jack flushed.

'I suppose I can't,' he replied, 'if you put it like that.'

'There is no other way to put it,' said the doctor, 'If some burglar broke into Mallory Hall and walked off with your most treasured possession, wouldn't you do your utmost to find the man? Of course you would, and quite rightly too. Well, the only difference is that you would set the law to work. These people will take the law into their own hands, and they won't even stick at murder to place the Black Idol back in the temple in which it belongs.'

Jack walked over to the porthole and gazed out thoughtfully. The sky on the horizon was flecked with red and gold, and a scintillating strip of crimson dyed the calm grey-blue of the sea. It was as though the water was dappled with blood, and he gave an involuntary shiver.

'All right, Dr. Hartley,' he said suddenly and turned, 'I'll follow your advice. It goes against the grain to go home empty-handed, but I'll do as you say.'

Dr. Hartley clapped him on the shoulders.

'Better go home empty-handed than

not go home at all,' he answered quietly. 'And believe me, Mallory, even if you did reach home with the idol, I doubt if you would ever know a minute's peace while it was in your possession. The Chinese are a tenacious race, and they'd follow you until they achieved their object. Ever since you told me the story last night, I've felt uneasy, and what happened a little while ago proves that my uneasiness was not without foundation I know the yellow race well, my boy. They are clever and cunning and determined.'

'Then you suggest that I leave the idol in such a position that this fellow, whoever he is, can get at it without any trouble?' said Jack.

'I do,' agreed Hartley. 'And if it hasn't gone by the time we reach London I further suggest that you take the first opportunity, after we leave the ship, to despatch it back to China. There is a man I know in Pekin who will see that it reaches its right destination.'

'I'll go back to my cabin now and take the thing out of its box,' said Jack Mallory resolutely. 'If I put it on the table by the bed and instruct the steward to leave the door open all day, that ought to do the trick.'

'If you wait a second while I slip on some clothes, I'll come with you,' said Hartley, as the young man stepped to the door, and Jack nodded.

The rim of the rising sun was peeping shyly above the skyline as they emerged on to the deck and walked along in the direction of Jack's cabin. There was still no one about for the ship had been sufficiently long at sea to render the sunrise, so attractive to so many passengers, during the first few days out, a stale form of amusement. Turning into the alley-way, however, on to which Mallory's door opened, Hartley thought he caught sight of a vague figure slipping up the companion-way that led to the boat-deck, but he said nothing, for he concluded that it was possibly one of the stewards. A second later he reconsidered this conclusion, for the door of Jack Mallory's cabin stood open, and the sight that met his gaze caused Dr. Hartley to start back with a suppressed cry of horror.

'Merciful heavens, look!' he muttered; and Jack, peering over his shoulder, went white to the lips.

Face upward on the floor lay the night steward, his mouth twisted into a grin of agony and terror, and it only needed a single glance to see that he was dead, for no human being could have lived with the wound that showed in his throat. It had been cut literally from ear to ear!

'I'm afraid you made your decision too late!' said Dr. Hartley, in a hushed voice, and pointed to the vacant place beneath the bunk.

The box containing the Black Idol had disappeared.

'This is terrible!' whispered Jack huskily. 'What had we better do?'

'We must inform the captain at once,' answered the doctor, 'and have every Chinaman in the ship searched. It shouldn't be a difficult task to find the murderer of this poor fellow, for the idol is too bulky to be easily concealed.'

But in this he was mistaken, for although every Chinaman on board was subjected to a rigid questioning and his belongings thoroughly overhauled, and every possible hiding-place on the ship searched, there was no sign of the Black Idol. It had vanished completely.

'And so far as you are concerned,' said Dr. Hartley, as he took leave of Jack at the docks, 'you can thank your lucky stars. You might quite easily have been the victim instead of that poor devil of a steward. What happened to the idol, heaven and the man who killed him alone know. I don't suppose either of us will ever see it again.'

He believed it when he spoke, but it was destined that both he and Jack Mallory were to see the Black Idol again, and under circumstances that neither of them would have dreamed of even in their wildest imaginings!

3

The Man Outside

It was some weeks before Dr. Hartley was able to keep his promise and spare the time for a visit to Mallory Hall, for an accumulation of business that he found awaiting him on his arrival back in London had kept him working at high pressure.

At last, however, he had succeeded in clearing up his arrears and with the prospect of a few days' leisure before him had decided to take advantage of Jack's invitation and run down into the country. His telegram had brought back a cordial reply from Sir Edward Mallory and towards the close of a hot summer's day Hartley's big open Rolls, with Eric, his son, at the wheel, ran swiftly through the old-world Sussex village of Market Hailsham, swung into the chestnut-lined drive of the rambling Tudor mansion that had been the home of the Mallorys for centuries and drew noiselessly to a halt in front of the weather-beaten oak door.

Rowson, the grey-haired butler who had grown old in the service of the family, emerged from the shadows of the arched entrance and greeted them with a smile of welcome on his round, florid face.

'This is a pleasure, Dr. Hartley,' he said in his soft, deferential voice — the perfect voice of a perfect butler. 'It is a long time now, sir, since you have paid us a visit.'

'A fault,' answered the doctor smiling, 'which I have many times promised myself that I would rectify, and at last here I am. How are you, Rowson? You're looking remarkably well.'

'Beyond a slight twinge of rheumatism now and again, sir,' said the butler, 'I am glad to say that I enjoy fairly good health. If you will come this way, sir, I will let Sir Edward know that you have arrived.'

He stood aside as Hartley mounted the broad flight of steps and entered the cool shadows of the big hall. He glanced round appreciatively at the suits of

armour, the coats-of-arms on the panelled walls, and the large stained-glass
window through which the dying rays of
the setting sun splashed vivid-hued
patterns on the mellow-coloured rugs
that strewed the polished floor.

'Just the same as ever,' he murmured.
'Nothing changed. Time seems to have
stood still here, Rowson.'

The butler sighed and a shadow
crossed his face.

'Times have changed, all the same, sir,'
he replied, shaking his grey head. 'I can
remember when the Hall was always full
of guests — Sir Edward used to be fond
of entertaining — but lately — ' He broke
off as a deep voice hailed them from the
top of the broad staircase.

'Hartley, begad!' it cried and a few
seconds later the doctor was shaking
hands vigorously with Sir Edward Mallory,
an older but all the same a startling repro-
duction of Jack. He possessed the same
deep blue eyes, the same thin-lipped mouth
and square jaw, and but for the fact that
age had slightly dimmed the blueness of
the eyes, drawn deeper lines about the

mouth, and silvered the wavy hair, might easily have passed for that young man's brother.

'Come into the library and have a spot of something to wash the dust of the roads out of your throat,' he said, taking the doctor by the arm. 'Then Rowson will show you to your rooms.'

They entered a large, lofty chamber on the right that was lined with books and filled with deep armchairs and loungers upholstered in dark-green leather. There were cabinets of priceless china, and the few pictures that graced the walls bore the signatures of famous artists.

'It was quite a coincidence that you should have been on the same ship as Jack,' said their host, pushing forward a couple of chairs. 'By Jove, that was an unpleasant experience, the murder of that poor steward! I suppose they never caught the chap who did it?'

Dr. Hartley shook his head. He had almost forgotten the incident in attending to a mass of other work.

'Not so far as I know,' he answered.

'It must have been one of those infernal

Chinamen,' said Sir Edward, waving his hand towards a box of cigars that stood on a table at the doctor's elbow. 'I'm jolly glad they got away with the idol, though. I was all against the idea from the first, in spite of the fact that it would have meant a lot to us if Jack had succeeded and found the jewels, but he insisted on having a try.' His face clouded for a moment. 'If that idol hadn't disappeared from his cabin in the way it did, I should have thought that the incidents that have been happening round here lately were connected with it.'

'What incidents are you referring to?' asked the doctor, pausing in the act of carefully clipping the end off his cigar.

'There have been one or two stories in the village of strangers having been seen in the neighbourhood at night,' answered the older man, 'and old Thompson, the postmaster, swears that he nearly ran into a Chinaman lurking in a lane on his way home from the local inn two nights ago. He wore a long cloak with a sort of hood. No doubt the fact that he had spent the evening at the Faithful Friend would account for that, but still I must admit that there may be something in it, for twice during the past three weeks an attempt has been made to break into this house.'

Dr. Hartley looked across at his host with an expression of interest in his deep-set eyes.

'Twice?' he murmured questioningly, and Sir Edward nodded.

'Yes,' he replied, 'and on each occasion he was disturbed before he could succeed in his object — once by Jack, who had come down here for a book and surprised the intruder at work on the catch of those windows' — he indicated the long French windows that had evidently been added as a modern improvement to the house at some time, and which overlooked a balcony — 'and the second time by myself. The night was very hot, and being unable to sleep I came down and went out into the garden to smoke a cigar and get a breath of cool air. I left the house by the small side door near the kitchen and strolled round towards the front. As I neared the dining room windows I saw a man spring up from a crouching position and make off down the drive.'

'I suppose you didn't see his face?' said Dr. Hartley, the furrow that had appeared between his brows denoting his interest.

'No,' answered Sir Edward. 'I'm under the impression that he wore a hood of some kind over his head, but I couldn't be sure. However, there was no doubt regarding his intention, for I found that a portion of the window had been almost cut out with a diamond, and the cutter was lying on the ground underneath. I informed the local police-inspector and he has put a man on duty to patrol the roads round the house since. As I say, if Jack had brought the idol home with him, I should put these incidents down to that. As it is, I conclude that they are just ordinary attempts at burglary.'

'It's certainly possible,' agreed the doctor, but his tone lacked conviction. 'The place contains sufficient valuables to tempt a thief, but it's distinctly unusual for burglars to be so persistent. Having been frightened away once, I should have thought they would have left the place alone.' He drew thoughtfully at his cigar and expelled a cloud of smoke. 'Have any rumours reached you since regarding strangers being seen in the vicinity?'

Eric, who up till now had been a silent and weary listener, thought it was time to interfere.

'Look here, guv'nor,' he broke in in an injured voice, 'I thought we'd come down for a few days' holiday, and now you're beginning to get all hot and bothered trying to nose out a mystery before we've properly got inside the front door.'

Hartley chuckled, and Sir Edward laughed outright.

Dr. Hartley's fondness for mysteries of any sort was well known both to his host and his son. Since he had retired from his Harley Street practice he had made a hobby of criminology, and anything in the nature of a crime attracted him like steel to a magnet.

'All right, Eric,' said the doctor good-humouredly, 'I won't ask any more questions. No doubt it was purely an ordinary attempt at burglary, and having tried twice and failed the burglars have given it up as hopeless and gone to find 'fresh fields and pastures new.' '

He began almost at once to chat about old times to their host and his son heaved a sigh of relief at having averted a catastrophe, for to spoil that brief oasis of rest in their busy lives seemed to him nothing less.

His relief would have been short-lived had he been gifted with the power of second sight, however, for before morning dawned the placid holiday to which he had looked forward was to be rudely disturbed. Already potent forces were focusing upon the little village, and Fate was even at that moment weaving a scarlet thread into the colourless wool of its history, for the converging plans of east and west were to meet at that peaceful spot, and meeting, change the lives of at least five of its inhabitants, and provide Dr. Hartley with a problem that for sheer horror and danger was unequalled by any that he had undertaken before.

Being mercifully unaware of the grim adventures that lay in store, Eric gave himself up to the pleasure of the present, and when later, after a hot bath, he had changed into a dinner-suit, he joined Dr. Hartley and Sir Edward Mallory in the dining room and was looking forward to his stay at the Hall with the keenest enjoyment.

'Where's Jack?' asked Hartley, as they seated themselves at one end of the massive dining-table.

'He won't be a minute,' answered Sir Edward. 'He's changing. The young rascal has been over to Haslemere and was late getting back.' He smiled slightly and there was a twinkle in his eye as he looked across at the doctor. 'I rather think that a certain young lady who has come to live there with her uncle is the attraction,' he added dryly, 'and really I'm not surprised. Jill Marsh is a remarkably pretty girl, and if I was a young man, begad, I'd be after her myself.'

Hartley remembered the tall, white-haired man and slim girl whom Jack had pointed out to him on the ship.

'You mean Professor Arlington's niece?' he remarked, and the elder man inclined his head. 'They came over on the same ship, and Jack mentioned that they were going to be neighbours.'

'They only moved in three weeks ago,' said Sir Edward, 'and for the past fortnight I haven't been quite sure whether this house or Haslemere is Jack's home. He certainly sleeps here, but that's about all.'

The subject of this rather exaggerated statement entered at that moment and smiled a cheery greeting.

'I'm awfully sorry I'm late,' he apologised seating himself opposite Hartley. 'My watch was slow.'

'You'd better have it seen to,' remarked his father. 'It's been getting slower and slower every night for a week.'

Jack coloured, and Hartley noted approvingly that he was looking much better than when he had seen him last. The drawn, furtive look had gone from his eyes, and his face was no longer pale, but healthily bronzed with the air and sun. The country or the proximity of the new neighbours had apparently done him good.

'I'm starving with hunger,' said Jack,

obviously hoping to divert their attention from his father's remark concerning the watch.

'Didn't they give you anything to eat at Haslemere?' asked Sir Edward innocently, and signed for Rowson to serve the soup.

'Er — yes, of course,' answered Jack sheepishly, his face the colour of a really choice tomato. 'But — er — I haven't had anything since — er — lunch. I — er — took Miss Marsh to show her the view from the top of Hangman's Hill this afternoon and we — er — forgot the time and — er — missed tea.'

'I suppose her watch was slow, too?' said Sir Edward gravely, and Eric felt convinced that it was only the arrival of the soup at that instant that saved Jack from an apoplectic stroke.

The meal was a merry one. Dr. Hartley was in his best form, and he and Sir Edward chatted away gaily, while Eric and Jack discussed a variety of subjects and found that their tastes were mostly similar.

Below the little party was a vast expanse of polished but empty mahogany, for the dining-table at Mallory Hall had in its time seated as many as thirty guests, and Rowson, when he entered with coffee, ponderous yet light-footed, seemed to emerge from a cavern of shadows, for the only light in the room was the shaded electric lamp in their midst.

'How many gardeners do you keep here?' asked Dr. Hartley suddenly apropos of nothing, and Sir Edward appeared slightly surprised.

'Five, I think,' he answered. 'Why?'

'That's a lot to find accommodation for,' said Hartley. 'Do they sleep on the premises?'

'Only the head-gardener,' answered his host, 'and he has a cottage near the road. I want you to try this port, Hartley,' he went on, as Rowson placed a decanter reverently before him. 'It's almost the last of the bin, and — '

But Dr. Hartley apparently wasn't the least interested in the port. He was gazing out through the big windows of the dining room, which were uncovered except for diaphanous casement curtains that draped the lower halves. The half light of dusk lay on the close-clipped lawn outside and the tall chestnut trees at the end of the shrubbery showed black against the deep blue of the sky. Nearer the house a mass of rhododendron bushes made a shadowy blot.

'What time do your gardeners finish work?' said the doctor, breaking in upon Sir Edward's praises of the port, and the elder man looked rather annoyed.

'They leave at seven o'clock,' he said a trifle testily. 'Have you suddenly taken up horticulture or — What the deuce is wrong, Hartley?'

Dr. Hartley had risen quickly and was walking to the door. There was a sharp click and the table light went out.

'Why — ' began Jack, but the doctor interrupted him.

'Stand back from the table against the wall, all of you!' he snapped in a harsh voice. 'I turned the light out. There's a man lurking in the shadow of those rhododendron bushes and he's got a gun!'

4

Startling News

Before the others had sufficiently recovered from the first shock of surprise to be able to offer any reply to his startling statement, Dr. Hartley had slipped out of the door and hurriedly crossing the hall, noiselessly unlatched the big main entrance. The dining room windows faced the same way as the front door, and when he came softly out on to the steps he was able to see the clump of bushes in the shadow of which he had noticed the lurking figure, by looking sideways to his right.

Keeping in the cover provided by the low hedge that bordered the drive he moved with incredible swiftness towards the lawn, but it was empty. The watcher by the rhododendrons had vanished. He paused for a second and listened, but there was no sound beyond the gentle rustle of the leaves as they stirred softly in the night wind. The lawn ended in a semi-circle of flowerbeds and behind these was the belt of chestnuts that marked the southern boundary of the estate. To the right was the fringe of a pine wood, and Hartley concluded that this was the only avenue of retreat that could have been taken by the intruder.

He went forward noiselessly until he reached the edge of the copse and once more stopped in the shelter of a tree-trunk to listen, but there was nothing to break the stillness of the night, and moving ahead again, he slipped quickly from tree to tree, his eyes straining to pierce the dusky gloom of the twilight. He was halfway through the little wood when he suddenly heard a faint sound in front of him scarcely fifty yards away. A little dry, choked cough! Someone was there ahead! With his pulses racing, Hartley started at a run towards the place from which he judged the cough had come. The trees here grew more thickly, and it was so dark that he couldn't see more than a few yards ahead, but now he could plainly distinguish the thud of retreating footsteps. The cougher had heard his approach, and was making off.

Hartley increased his pace, and then suddenly the sounds in front stopped, and almost instantly from the darkness ahead came a sharp stab of flame. Plop! Hartley flung himself to the ground, and the bullet thudded into the trunk of a tree behind him.

Plop! Plop! Two more shots in quick succession followed, and, by the dull report like the drawing of a cork, the doctor knew that the sniper's pistol was fitted with a silencer.

Plop! The fourth bullet smacked into the ground, and was too near his face to be pleasant. Hartley wriggled his way sideways until he was behind the shelter of a massive pine-tree, and then cautiously straightened up.

Three more shots pattered among the tree-trunks, but from the erratic placing of the bullets, the doctor guessed that the shooter had lost track of him.

With a grim smile curving the corners of his mouth, he began stealthily to advance, taking a semi-circular route. The thick carpet of pine-needles under his feet made his movements noiseless, and every few paces he stopped and listened. His unseen adversary had not moved, and Hartley almost chuckled at the success of his plan. The unknown was still waiting for some sound that would enable him to locate the doctor, and in the meanwhile, Hartley was drawing steadily nearer and preparing to take him by surprise from the rear!

In a little while he was able to make out a dim blot of shadow — a mere smudge against the paler shadow of the dusk. Carefully using every precaution to avoid disturbing his quarry, Dr. Hartley drew nearer and nearer. He was within four yards of his man now, and could see him plainly — a half-crouching figure, peering forward, motionless, intent, listening!

Hartley crept towards him, and then, when barely a yard separated them, he launched himself forward and sprang on the other's back.

With a snarling cry the man twisted round, and they both fell heavily rolling over and over and clawing desperately for a hold. It was a tooth and nail fight, and what might have been the result is open to conjecture. The unknown was exceptionally strong, but Hartley would probably have got the better of him if luck hadn't taken a hand in his favour.

Twisting and writhing, they suddenly brought up sharply against the trunk of a tree. At least, it was the doctor's head that first discovered that it was there, and the blow all but stunned him. For a moment he relaxed his hold, and in that second his opponent jerked himself free, and, leaping to his feet, went racing off through the wood.

Feeling sick and dizzy, Hartley scrambled to his knees, his head aching furiously, and it was several seconds before he could stand. By the time he had staggered out of the wood into the open, there was not a soul in sight. The man with the pistol had got clean away. Thoroughly annoyed with himself for having lost his quarry, Hartley looked about him. The wood separated the gardens of Mallory Hall from the meadows, but although he gazed in every direction, nothing moved, and presently he turned.

He had retraced his steps halfway through the wood when he heard the sound of feet hurriedly approaching, and guessed it was Eric before he saw the white shirt-fronts emerge from the darkness. Jack was behind his son, and he panted a question as they came running up to Hartley.

'I saw him all right,' replied the doctor grimly, 'and I felt him too. In fact, but for a piece of infernal luck, I should have got the better of the fellow.'

'Who was it?' asked Jack rather stupidly.

'My dear fellow, how the deuce should I know?' snapped Hartley irritably. 'He forgot to leave me his visiting-card. Who ever he was, he was up to no good.'

They walked on in silence for a few seconds, Hartley deep in thought, Jack and Eric frankly puzzled and curious.

'How did you know he'd got a gun in this light?' ventured Eric at last. 'I mean when you saw him from the window.'

'I saw it gleam,' answered the doctor, 'saw the light on it. It couldn't have been anything else but a gun.'

'But what the dickens was he doing

there at all?' asked the bewildered Jack. 'Hiding in the bushes with a gun — what for?'

'I'd like to know that,' said Hartley. 'One thing, however, I'm sure of.'

'What's that?' said Eric.

'These attempts at breaking in that Mallory was telling us about this evening,' answered the doctor, 'they are certainly not the work of ordinary burglars. This episode to-night proves it. It is too big a strain on the imagination to suppose that these events are unconnected.'

'Has my father been telling you about the man I saw trying to get in by the library window?' asked the young man.

'Yes,' replied Hartley, 'and also the man he surprised by the dining room window. Somebody is very anxious to get into Mallory Hall, my boy, and the question is — what for?'

'I can think of nothing,' said Jack, shaking his head, 'unless — '

He stopped.

'Unless what?' demanded Hartley quickly.

'Did father tell you what Thompson,

the postmaster, says he saw?' said Jack softly.

'The hooded Chinaman?' inquired the doctor.

'Yes.'

'Well, do you think that these incidents can have anything to do with the Black Idol?'

The young man made the suggestion hesitantly, as though he was afraid of ridicule.

'It certainly crossed my mind,' admitted Hartley thoughtfully, 'but I really don't see how they can. For one thing, you haven't got the idol. The person who killed the steward got that, or presumably so, for it disappeared at the same time. And, for another, the man who was watching the house to-night was not a Chinaman.'

'Are you sure of that?'

There was a note of relief in Jack's voice as he put the question.

'Perfectly,' said Hartley emphatically. 'I couldn't see his face sufficiently clear to recognise him again, but enough to know that he was of the white races.'

'Then I don't understand it at all,' said Jack. 'It's a mystery.'

The doctor relapsed into silence, and they didn't speak again until they reached the lawn and found Sir Edward waiting for them, pacing impatiently up and down, puffing at his cigar.

He listened attentively while the doctor briefly related what had happened, and when he had finished, shrugged his shoulders.

'I don't understand it,' he said unconsciously echoing his son. 'Unless these fellows are after the plate or the pictures, there's nothing at Mallory Hall to tempt them — there's certainly no money.'

'I am convinced that there is more in it than ordinary burglary,' declared Hartley. 'But we can't do anything more for the moment. It would be as well to get in touch with the police and warn them of this occurrence, and then we must just wait and see if there are any more developments.'

'Do you think there will be, guv'nor?' asked Eric quickly.

'I do, Eric,' replied the doctor. 'I know no more about this business or what's at the bottom of it than you do, but I'm willing to wager that something else happens before very long.'

He spoke prophetically, for the last word had barely left his lips when they heard the sound of running feet coming up the drive.

'Who the deuce can this be?' muttered Sir Edward, gazing down the dark avenue.

The hurried footsteps drew nearer, and they heard the sound of sobbing breath mingled with the patter on the gravel, then round the bend, stumbled a figure — the figure of a girl in evening dress.

'Good heavens, Jill!' cried Jack and sprang forward to meet her.

She clung to his arm piteously as he reached her side, and her breath came in deep, uneven gasps.

'What's the matter?' he asked anxiously. 'What are you doing here?'

She tried to speak but no words came, and Dr. Hartley saw, with a thrill of horror, that the front of her dress and one of her bare arms was smothered in blood!

'She's hurt!' he cried crisply. 'Look here!'

He stepped forward, but she waved him back.

'I'm — not — hurt,' she gasped painfully. 'It's — my — uncle!' Her voice trailed away in a husky whisper.

'Your uncle?' said Jack, his arm round her. 'What's the matter with him?'

'I — found — him — dead — in — his — study,' she answered with a supreme effort. 'There was — blood — on the desk — ' She gave a shudder, uttered a little moan, and went limp in Jack's arms.

'You'd better bring her into the house,' said Dr. Hartley. 'She's fainted!'

5

Shots In the Night

They carried the unconscious girl into the library and laid her on a settee, and while Jack went in search of water Hartley gently chafed her wrists.

Sir Edward stood by, a frown on his brow.

'Something pretty terrible must have happened at Haslemere to have reduced her to this state,' he remarked as Jack came back with a glass of water.

The doctor nodded, and raised the girl's head.

'You heard what she said,' he answered. 'Her uncle has met with some kind of accident. I think as soon as she has recovered, we'd better go over and find out what has occurred.'

A faint fleeting sigh escaped her clenched teeth and her compressed lips parted. Jack forced a few drops of the water between them, and after a few minutes she opened her eyes. She gazed vacantly about her with an expression of bewilderment, and then, as memory returned, the look of bewilderment changed to one of horror.

'My — my uncle,' she faltered tremulously. 'The knife — ' She tried to struggle up and succeeded with the help of Jack's arm.

'What happened?' asked the young man as she pressed a shaking hand across her forehead.

'Oh, it was horrible!' she gasped incoherently. 'I — went into uncle's study — to see if he wanted anything — and found him — lying across the writing-table — there was a knife — in his back — the papers were all over blood.' She shivered, and her voice faded to silence.

Hartley shot a quick, significant look at Eric. The mysterious happenings of that night had apparently piled themselves up to a horrible climax.

'Did you inform the police?' he asked and Jill shook her head, weakly.

'No,' she answered. 'I don't know what

I did. I called to Briggs and then I hurried over here. I thought that Jack — ' She stopped, leaving the sentence unfinished.

'I think,' said Hartley crisply, 'that it would be as well if Eric and I went over to Haslemere at once. It appears to be a case of murder, and therefore we should waste no time in telling the police what has happened.'

'I agree with you,' said Sir Edward gravely. 'There is a short cut through the home covert that will bring you to the house in less than ten minutes. Jack can stay here and bring Miss Marsh back when she is better, and if you like I'll come with you and show you the way.'

'An excellent idea,' assented Dr. Hartley.

He turned to the white-faced girl who had relapsed on to the cushions, her slim form shuddering every now and again from the nervous strain resulting from the shock she had received.

'We will look after everything, Miss Marsh,' he said gently; and then in a lower tone to Jack: 'What she wants is a good stiff dose of bromide and a long rest

— in fact the best thing you can do is to arrange for her to stay the night here.'

'I'll see Mrs. Henderson,' answered the young man. 'You leave Jill to me — I'll look after her.'

Sir Edward rang the bell and sent Rowson, who answered the summons, for the housekeeper, and then, with a word of farewell to the girl and Jack, they set off for Haslemere.

A sliver of moon hung in the deep indigo of the sky, and its faint light enabled them to see fairly clearly. Sir Edward led the way across the lawn to the little pine wood through which Hartley had chased the armed marauder shortly before, and as they entered the gloomy depths the doctor wondered what connection, if any, there was between the watcher on the lawn and this latest development. The peaceful old country house of the Mallorys seemed to have become the focus point for dark and mysterious happenings, and even the beauty of the surroundings took on a sinister aspect.

When they reached the end of the

wood and came out into the clearing, Sir Edward turned sharply to the right, and steered them through a small gate set in a barbed wire fence that ran parallel with a ploughed field. Away to the left were a succession of meadows that stretched to a distant slope of wooded hillside and ahead a narrow footpath that twisted through a straggling belt of trees and finally emerged upon a lane which was evidently little used, for the tall hedges that lined either side almost met, and they had to force the branches aside as they proceeded. Half-way along the lane was a stile, and climbing this, they found themselves within sight of a long low building of white stone the ground floor windows of which blazed with light.

'Haslemere,' said their host briefly, and a few seconds later they emerged from a thicket, and, passing through a clump of evergreens, came out on to a broad gravelled drive.

'We've saved nearly two miles by coming this way,' said Sir Edward as they walked swiftly towards the front entrance.

The double doors were open and a tall

thin, scared-looking man in the conventional black of an upper servant stood on the threshold, while behind him in the lighted hall clustered an agitated group of men and women talking and whispering among themselves.

'What's happened here, Briggs?' called Sir Edward, as they approached within earshot, and the tall butler came to meet them.

'A terrible thing, sir!' the man quavered hoarsely. 'The master has been killed — stabbed! Miss Jill found him, sir, and called me. I've been trying to get on to the police, but the telephone won't work.'

'Won't work!' interrupted Dr. Hartley sharply.

'No, sir,' answered the butler. 'I couldn't get any reply from the exchange. I've sent the second footman down to Hailsham on to his bicycle.' He turned a troubled face to Sir Edward. 'I don't know what's happened to Miss Jill,' he said, 'I can't find her any — '

'She's all right, Briggs,' Sir Edward assured him. 'She's over at the Hall. It was she who first let us know that there was anything wrong here.'

'It's a dreadful business, sir,' began Briggs but Hartley again interrupted him.

'I should like to have a look at the study at once,' he said, and then, seeing the expression of doubt that came over the butler's face: 'It's all right, Briggs, Sir Edward will vouch for my bona fides. My name is James Hartley, and although I am not officially connected with the police, I have some experience of these affairs.'

The doubtful look cleared from the butler's face as Sir Edward Mallory substantiated the doctor's claim with a nod.

'I shall be only too glad, sir,' he said fervently, 'if you will take the responsibility from my shoulders. I've never been mixed up in anything like this before, and it's upset me so that I don't know whether I'm on my head or my heels.'

'You've done very well up to now,' said Dr. Hartley. 'If you will show us the way to the study, I can have a look round before the police arrive, and so save any more delay.'

Without another word, Briggs turned

and led the way up the steps into the hall. Followed by the curious eyes of the other servants grouped at the foot of the stairs, he crossed to a door on the right and bending down, unlocked it.

'I locked the door directly I knew what had happened, sir,' he explained, and opened the door gently and stood aside for them to enter.

Dr. Hartley was the first to step across the threshold of the room of death, and as his eyes took in the scene before him Eric heard him give a low exclamation. Standing at his elbow, the lad peered over the doctor's shoulder, and his breathing quickened as he saw the reason for Hartley's involuntary cry.

The room was large, and built in the shape of a hexagon. Facing the door was a pair of high French windows that reached almost from the ceiling to the floor, and these were open. At an angle in front of them was a massive, flat-topped desk of age-old, black oak. The surface was littered with books and papers, and sprawling in the midst of this muddle, was a white-haired man, his arms spread out across the desk, one hand gripping a bunch of papers. He was in evening-dress, and from between his shoulder blades protruded the carved handle of a knife!

Dr. Hartley let his eyes rest on him for perhaps a minute, and then, without moving from his position just within the doorway, he took stock of the rest of the room.

The walls were lined with dwarf bookcases filled with volumes of all shapes and sizes — some new — others obviously very old. Here and there the regular line of bookshelves was broken by tall cabinets containing a collection of Chinese curios arranged in orderly array.

The pictures were nearly all Chinese prints and framed tapestries, with the exception of a large photograph of Jill Marsh that stood at one corner of the writing-table. This room where tragedy had come so swiftly and so suddenly was evidently the working place of a student.

A light-covered carpet covered the floor, and from the open window to a high embroidered screen that masked one side of the fireplace ran a double line of muddy footprints. The doctor looked at these in perplexity, his brows drawn together in a frown. There had been no rain for several days, and yet the person who made those marks had obviously walked over muddy ground.

With a word to Eric and the others to remain where they were, Hartley went over to the writing-table, taking care to avoid the footprints on the carpet. Stooping over the motionless figure that lay face-downwards over the blotting pad, he gave it and the table a swift scrutiny. The papers and manuscript near the body were splashed and splattered with crimson, and it was not until the doctor tried to raise the dead man in order to see his face that the reason for this large amount of blood became evident. The knife that had killed him had been driven with such force that it had passed completely through the body, pinning it to a card.

'Whoever killed Arlington must have been the possessor of prodigious strength,' he murmured letting the dead man drop gently back into his original position. 'The muscle necessary for a blow like that would be enormous.' He looked across at Briggs, who was standing nervously in the doorway. 'Tell me exactly how the discovery was made,' he said.

The butler hesitated and moistened his lips.

'The first intimation I had that anything was wrong, sir,' he said in a low voice, 'was when I heard Miss Jill cry out. The master had gone to his study and had been there about an hour. Miss Jill had told him during dinner that she was tired and was going to bed early, and I think she must have gone to say goodnight. I was in the dining room when I heard her scream out and, hurrying out, I saw her leaning against the door-post, white as a sheet. She just pointed and whispered, 'Briggs, look! Phone for the police,' and then she ran across the room and out by the open windows.'

'Where were you during the time your master was in the study?' asked Hartley.

'Part of the time I was in the kitchen,' replied the butler, 'but mostly putting things away in the dining room.'

'Where is the dining room?'

'On the opposite side of the hall, sir,'

'And you heard no sound from here at all?'

The butler shook his head.

'No, sir,' he answered, 'except that about a quarter of an hour before Miss Jill's cry, I heard a noise which I thought was the closing of a door.'

'The closing of a door!' repeated Dr. Hartley. 'Which door — the study door?'

'No, sir,' said Briggs, 'it sounded more like one of those cabinet doors. It was just a faint squeak and thud.'

'Humph!' The doctor stroked his chin thoughtfully and his eyes strayed to the marks on the carpet. 'It seems fairly evident that the murderer came in by way of the windows. That gives us two alternatives. Either he was someone well known to Arlington and therefore his appearance occasioned the professor neither surprise nor alarm, or — and I'm inclined to think this is a great deal more likely — he had already entered the room and was concealed behind that screen when Arlington came in after dinner.'

'But where did the mud come from, guv'nor?' asked Eric. 'There hasn't been any rain, so — '

'I was wondering about that myself, young 'un,' broke in the doctor. 'Probably — '

'I think I can explain that, sir,' said the butler quickly. 'The master was having some flower-beds made at the end of the lawn, and Williams, the gardener, sir, was planting seeds all the afternoon. Just before he went home, he gave the new beds a thorough watering.'

'That will be it,' agreed Dr. Hartley, nodding. 'We shall have to take a look at those beds. There are probably traces in the mould that will help us. In the meanwhile — '

He stopped short in the middle of his sentence, raising his head with a jerk. From outside clear and distinct in the stillness of the night, and at no great distance away, came the sound of a shot, followed almost immediately by two others in rapid succession!

6

The Hooded Raider

Dr. Hartley was at the windows almost before the echoes of the first report had died away.

'Come on, Eric!' he snapped crisply over his shoulder, as he went out on to the balcony. 'I'm going to find out the meaning of those shots.'

'I expect it's a poacher,' said the lad, as he followed at the doctor's heels.

'Poachers don't use automatics,' retorted Hartley, 'and those shots came from an automatic, or I'm a Dutchman.'

He ran quickly down the stone steps that led from the balcony to the lawn and paused to get his bearings.

'The shooting was somewhere over there, I think,' he said, pointing towards a belt of trees that rose black against the night sky at the end of the close-cropped plot of grass. 'It may have been a little farther away, but I don't think so.'

He set off with long strides walking at a pace that forced Eric to break into a run to keep up with him.

The distance to the trees proved deceptive in the faint light of the crescent moon, for by the time they reached the centre of the lawn, they seemed to be as far away as ever. Presently they came to the newly-made flower-beds that the butler had mentioned. They stretched between the end of the lawn and a broad expanse of thick shrubbery.

Hartley stopped and took a torch from his pocket.

'We've got to be careful here,' he warned. 'I don't want to destroy any traces that the murderer may have left in the earth, and at the same time I'm not particularly keen to provide the gentleman owning the automatic with a target on which to practise his shooting.'

He flashed on the light and fanned it over the ground and then with a little grunt of satisfaction he snapped it off again.

'It's all right,' he muttered. 'There are

no prints at this particular spot so we can proceed without worrying.'

He picked his way carefully over the soft mould and, reaching the outskirts of the bushes beyond, paused and listened. Not a sound broke the stillness except from somewhere far away the long wail of a train whistle sounded.

Satisfied that there was nobody about, Dr. Hartley began to force his way through the rhododendrons, Eric following closely behind him. The shrubbery occupied a large patch of ground, but presently they came out into a clearing where the bushes grew less thickly. A few yards away was the beginning of a wood. Hartley switched on his torch again, and almost the first thing he saw, as the circle of light swept the ground, was a spent cartridge shell. He picked it up.

'This is undoubtedly the spot from whence those shots were fired, Eric,' he said and, searching round, found another shell a few feet away from the first. He was looking for the third cartridge, when a cry from Eric attracted his attention, and he looked up quickly.

'Look — there!' exclaimed the lad, and, following the direction of his pointing finger, the doctor caught sight of something that protruded from a clump of isolated bushes.

Turning the ray of his torch-light on to it, he saw with a little creepy chill in the region of his spine that it was a foot! It projected at an awkward angle — the booted foot of a man, motionless and lifeless.

Dr. Hartley hurried over to this gruesome object and parting the branches of the concealing evergreens, compressed his lips grimly at the thing he revealed.

Face downwards lay the still figure of a man, an ominous stain of blood soaking the back of the dark hooded cloak he was wearing!

'Death seems to have been very busy in this neighbourhood to-night,' murmured the doctor softly, and, handing his torch to Eric, he dropped down on his knees beside the body and gently turned it over. A startled cry escaped his lips as the light of the torch fell full upon the dead face — the man was a Chinaman!

'Gosh!' ejaculated Eric in astonishment. 'A Chinese!'

Dr. Hartley nodded.

'And also the man who raided Arlington's house and killed him,' he said, as he scrutinised the body keenly.

'What makes you think that, guv'nor?' asked the lad.

The doctor pointed to the feet.

'There are still traces of wet mould from the flower-beds adhering to the soles of his boots,' he answered and unbuttoning the cloak he placed his hand in the region of the heart. 'He's quite dead,' he continued, 'apparently shot in the back. Now the question is, how was he killed, and who killed him?'

'And also why did he murder Arlington?' said Eric.

'I have a vague idea to account for that,' said Hartley to the other's surprise. 'But I must admit that I'm completely in the dark as to why he was himself killed.'

He had been rapidly feeling in the dead man's pockets while speaking, and now he passed his fingers quickly over the upper part of the arms.

'There's nothing in his pockets,' he announced, 'but if you put your hand here, and here' — he touched the man's arms — 'I think you'll agree that there's no doubt he was responsible for the death of the professor.'

The lad obeyed, and felt the hard, bulging muscles that stood out like huge knots under the sleeve.

'Great Scot!' he gasped. 'He must have been tremendously strong.'

'And it was a tremendously strong man who drove that knife into Arlington's back,' said Dr. Hartley. 'Nobody except a person of abnormal strength could have caused the weapon to pass clean through the body as it did. That's why I'm fairly certain that this fellow was the murderer.'

He rose to his feet, and stood looking down at the sprawling figure thoughtfully. Who had killed him and why? Death must have come swiftly and unexpectedly, for the expression on the yellow face was one of startled surprise. He had probably never even known what it was that had struck him down. Who other than the Chinaman had been lurking in the

71

vicinity that night? Was it the man whom Hartley had encountered in the pine wood, the man who had been watching Mallory Hall from the lawn — and, if so, what was his object?

The presence of the Chinaman suggested the possibility that the Black Idol was at the bottom of the mystery, and, if that were the case, then who had taken it from Jack's cabin and killed the steward? Certainly not the Chinese emissaries of the priests of the Temple of Tsao-Sun, as the doctor had at first supposed, for in that case they would not still be chasing it. Who then? There was only one answer to that question, after the events of the night — unless the dead Chinaman and the rest of the tragic happenings were entirely unconnected with the Black Idol — and that was Arlington!

On the face of it, it seemed scarcely conceivable that an eminent man like the late professor would have stooped to murder and theft, yet he had been killed, and by the Chinaman who lay so still and motionless at Hartley's feet. Supposing, for the sake of argument, that Arlington had stolen the image, it provided a motive for his murder, and also explained why Jack had been left unmolested.

Hartley had reached this stage in his reasoning when he suddenly remembered the two attempts to break into Mallory Hall, and his theory tumbled to the ground like a house of cards. If Arlington had had the idol in his possession, what was the explanation of these two attempted burglaries? Had the real whereabouts of the image only just become known? And then there was the man in the wood. He had been a European — a white man. How did he come into it?

These questions raced swiftly through Hartley's mind, but he could find no convincing answers, and with a slight irritable shrug of his shoulders, he turned to Eric.

'I don't think we can do very much more here,' he said. 'We'll just have a quick look round, in case there is anything that may help us, and then the best thing will be for you to remain here while I go back to the house and see if the police have arrived.'

He took the torch from the lad's hand and swept it over the ground, beginning close to the body of the dead Chinaman and gradually moving away in ever-widening circles. But though he searched carefully, there was nothing to reward his diligence. The man who had fired those fatal shots had left no traces behind other than the spent shells, the third of which he found at the foot of a large oak-tree.

It was Eric who made the only discovery worth while, and even that, at the moment, conveyed nothing to either of them.

The lad was watching Hartley, when his eyes caught sight of something white half-hidden in a tuft of rank grass. He picked it up and found that it was a torn scrap of paper, slightly crumpled, but otherwise clean and new, and had evidently not been lying there long. It was a corner apparently torn from a larger sheet, and bore the single word 'Moat' written on it in ink. The ink was fresh, and Dr. Hartley examined it carefully, when Eric drew his attention to it, but shook his head.

'I can't make anything of it at present,' he said. 'It may have nothing whatever to do with this business at all. However, I'll keep it in case.'

He stowed it away in his pocket-book.

'I'll get back to the house now,' he remarked. 'Stay here, Eric, until I send a constable to take charge.'

The police, in the person of a large inspector and bucolic constable of uncertain age, had arrived when he got back, and were in the study talking to Sir Edward Mallory and the dazed and frightened butler.

'This is a most mysterious business, Sir,' said Inspector Parrish, when the doctor was introduced to him. 'An extraordinary affair altogether.'

Hartley agreed with him, and without further preliminary recounted his discovery of the dead Chinaman in the shrubbery.

Sir Edward and the Inspector listened, the latter's face expressing a mixture of frowning thought and amazed perplexity.

'This seems to be a regular scorcher,'

he remarked at the end of the doctor's story. 'A Chinaman!'

He scratched his head, looking obviously out of his depth. To a man accustomed to dealing with poachers and the occasional robbery of a chicken run, the sudden advent of two murders breaking into the peace of his uneventful life had left him gasping like a fish out of water. The simile was, thought Hartley with a suppressed smile, rather apt, since Inspector Parrish resembled nothing so much as a large and well-fed cod!

'I'd better go and have a look at this fellow,' said the inspector heavily, 'You say you found him in the shrubbery at the end of the lawn, sir?'

Hartley nodded, and explained the exact position of the body.

'You'll find my son on guard,' he said, 'and when you relieve him, you might ask him to come back here.'

'I will.' The inspector turned to the aged and stolid constable. 'You'd better come with me,' he said, 'and after I've completed my investigations of this other crime I'll come back 'ere and 'ave a word with the servants.'

He departed majestically through the French windows followed by his subordinate, and when they had gone Sir Edward turned to Dr. Hartley.

'What do you make of this shocking business?' he said in a low voice. 'The finding of that dead Chinaman seems to bear out Thompson's story of the hooded man he saw lurking about the lane that night, doesn't it?'

Hartley nodded.

'Yes, I don't think he was mistaken,' he replied. 'As to what do I make of it all, that's soon told. I don't make anything of it yet.'

He kept his vague suspicion regarding Arlington and the Black Idol to himself. After all, it was only a suspicion, and though to a certain extent it covered the facts, Hartley felt chary of putting it into words and besmirching the dead man's memory until he had more definite proof to go on. It was altogether rather an impossible and far-fetched theory when considered clearly.

Sir Edward however, had been thinking

things over for himself.

'You know, it's an extraordinary coincidence, Hartley,' he said musingly, 'Arlington being a recognised authority on everything Chinese, and your finding the dead Chinaman in those bushes, and the Black Idol, and — everything.' He stopped rather lamely and looked at his friend.

'In what way — a coincidence?' asked the doctor.

'Well, I mean' — Sir Edward hesitated — 'Arlington was on that boat when the image disappeared, and now he's been murdered, and obviously by a Chinaman — there must be some connection.'

'But who killed the Chinaman?' said Dr. Hartley. 'If you're suggesting, as I suppose you are, that Arlington stole the Black Idol from Jack's cabin and brought it here, and that he was killed in order to regain possession of it, who shot his murderer?'

Sir Edward frowned and shook his head, but remained silent.

'And who cut the throat of that unfortunate steward?' the doctor went on.

'Arlington may have descended to theft to possess himself of such a unique specimen of Chinese art and legend as the Black Idol, but I don't think he would go so far as murder. And even supposing, for the sake of argument, that he did, how do the attempts to break into Mallory Hall fit in? and the man who shot at me in the wood?'

'I haven't the least idea,' said Sir Edward candidly. 'It was only while I was turning things over in my mind that the idea struck me.'

'It occurred to me, too,' admitted Hartley, 'but there are so many things against it that it's scarcely worth considering even as a working hypothesis.'

He began a systematic and careful examination of the room, but found nothing to throw any further light on the mystery. There were indications behind the screen that someone — undoubtedly the murderer — had been concealed there for a considerable period, but that was all. Presumably the Chinaman had entered by the French windows while the room was empty, and had hidden himself behind the screen on hearing. Arlington approaching. It seemed strange that the professor hadn't noticed the muddy footmarks on the carpet; but this was explainable when the butler, Briggs, asserted that his master had suffered from extreme shortness of sight. The question was what had the Chinaman come for? Certainly not for the Black Idol, as if he had, he had gone away empty-handed for there was no place in which the image could have been concealed, and a question to the butler elicited the reply that he had never seen anything like it.

The first tangible clue, curiously enough, came all unconsciously from Inspector Parrish. He returned with Eric just as Hartley had finished his investigations.

'It's a queer business,' he said blowing his nose violently, 'a very queer business. It looks to me as that Chinaman had been taking a short cut to the station when he was killed.'

'The station?' queried Hartley. 'Do you

mean the railway station?'

Inspector Parrish nodded.

'Yes,' he replied. 'Just beyond that shrubbery there's a narrow lane that runs past the Moat Farm and connects with a road leading direct to the station.'

Dr. Hartley scarcely heard the end of the sentence. His mind had fastened on two words: the 'Moat Farm.' 'Moat' was the word on that scrap of paper he had found beside the Chinaman's dead body, and he decided mentally that the Moat Farm would be worth a visit at the earliest opportunity.

He said nothing; but waiting until the inspector had begun his examination of the servants, he beckoned to Eric and drew the lad on one side.

'I'm going along to have a look at this place they call the Moat Farm,' he said in a low voice.

'Can I come with you?' asked the lad eagerly, and his face dropped when the other shook his head.

'No, I think you'd better stay here,' said the doctor. 'It may only be a wild goose chase, after all, and that piece of paper have been dropped by quite an innocent person. But it's worth following up.'

The inspector was questioning one of the maids, a quite unnecessary proceeding since the girl obviously knew nothing regarding the tragedy, and Dr. Hartley, taking advantage of his preoccupation, slipped away in search of Briggs.

He found the butler hovering nervously about the hall.

'Which is the way to Moat Farm?' he asked casually.

Briggs opened his eyes wide and stared at Hartley speechlessly.

'The Moat Farm!' he stammered at length. 'You're not thinking of going there, surely, sir?'

'Why not?' snapped the doctor sharply, and the butler shook his head.

'It's not a pleasant place at night, sir,' he replied hoarsely. 'It's been empty for years, and there are stories in the village — '

Hartley laughed at the butler's serious tone.

'I'll risk that,' he said lightly. 'Now

which is the way?'

With a resigned air, as one who had done his best and failed, Briggs supplied him with brief directions, and Dr. Hartley set off, little dreaming of what awaited him at the end of the journey.

7

At the Moat Farm

It was a beautiful night without a breath of wind, the moon, a shaving of silver set in blue enamel, and Dr. Hartley had no difficulty in finding the lane that the butler had described. It was little more than a cart-track, and obviously seldom used, for the surface was full of pits and holes, and the doctor had to pick his way with care.

As he strode briskly along, his mind was fully occupied with the problem that had been pitchforked into his holiday like a bolt from the blue. The more he thought about it, the more clearly did it become evident that in some way or other the Black Idol was at the bottom of the whole business, but how he couldn't make up his mind. To understand that it was necessary to know who had stolen the image in the first place from Jack

Mallory's cabin, and, what had happened to it subsequently. That Arlington might have been the culprit so far as the theft was concerned was conceivable, but that the professor should have murdered the steward was absurd. In which case, Arlington could have had nothing to do with the matter at all, for it was equally as absurd to suppose that whoever had cut the throat of the steward hadn't also taken the idol, otherwise there was no motive for the crime.

Dr. Hartley tried vainly to reduce the whole series of incidents to a concrete pattern — the murder of the steward, the disappearance of the idol, the Chinaman seen lurking in the lanes around Hailsham, the attempts to break into Mallory Hall, the man in the wood, the murder of Arlington, and the dead body of the shot Chinaman. These were the pieces of the jigsaw that were waiting to be fitted together to form a complete picture. The trouble was that they didn't fit — not any of them. There were either too many or not enough. The central piece, without which the rest of the design could not possibly be dropped into place, was missing — the Black Idol.

The lane along which he was walking presently entered an avenue of tall, closely-growing trees, which shut off the pale light of the crescent moon, and made the darkness so intense that Hartley was forced to switch his thoughts from conjecture to facts, and concentrate the whole of his senses on avoiding the ruts and potholes. The atmosphere, too, had subtly changed. The clear, sweet air of the night had given place to a dank, evil-smelling odour redolent of rotting vegetation. There was something the reason for which he couldn't define, about this sudden change of atmosphere that caused Hartley to shiver. It was as though somebody had run an ice-cold hand down his spine. Without pausing, however, he stumbled on, repressing a desire to pull his torch from his pocket and light his way. He concluded that he must be getting very near to Moat Farm by now, although so far as he could see there was no sign of a building of any sort and a light would undoubtedly give warning of his approach to anyone the place contained.

About fifty yards farther on the cart-track swung sharply to the left, and close in front Hartley got his first view of Moat Farm. He stopped, and surveyed it with mixed feelings, and came to the conclusion that a more depressing-looking place he had never seen.

It was surrounded by tall trees except on the side towards which he was looking and there lay a large pool of black stagnant and unruffled water; no doubt the pool had given the place its name. The house itself was low and rambling, and drifted away into numerous broken-down and ramshackle outbuildings. It seemed to squat amid the trees like a dead thing in the first stages of corruption. No gleam of light came from any window; no sound broke the absolute stillness, and the whole scene gave the impression of being steeped in indescribable gloom.

Dr. Hartley stood for a moment taking in every detail of this unprepossessing picture, and then decided to have a closer view. Skirting the silent pool, he approached the house, wading knee-deep in rank undergrowth. Broken wooden steps covered with weeds led up to the porch, which was overhung with ivy and trailing creepers.

For a moment the doctor hesitated, then he went up the steps cautiously and tried the door. To his surprise it gave under his hand. As well as being unlocked, it was not even latched, but swung over as he touched it.

Dr. Hartley held it half-ajar and listened. The place looked deserted and sounded deserted, but that open door was peculiar. He listened, straining his ears to catch the slightest sound from the dark interior, but there was nothing only a faint scurrying which he put down to rats.

After an appreciable hesitation, he crossed the threshold noiselessly and entered the hall. In the dim light that filtered through a grimy window on his left, he saw a chair, a broken table, and the beginning of a flight of stairs that led upwards.

The dust was thick everywhere. It rose in choking clouds and deadened the sound of his feet as he crept a few paces forward. It was like walking on a thick pile carpet, and it struck him that the house must have been empty for years. Again he paused and listened, and this time he thought he detected a faint sound from somewhere above — a muffled hum like the whispering of voices.

He stared at the dim outline of the staircase fading into utter darkness. He could see fairly clearly in the hall, for his eyes were growing accustomed to the gloom, but up above the blackness was absolute. Should he ascend those stairs and try to discover from whence came that low, sibilant murmur, or should he go back and fetch the inspector and Eric! It didn't take him long to make up his mind. By the time he had returned to Haslemere, and got back again with reinforcements, the occupants of the Moat Farm, whoever they were, would have ample time to clear out. He decided to go forward on his own.

On tiptoe he crossed the hall to the foot of the stairs. A mouldering carpet covered them in patches, a decaying legacy of the former tenants, and he began to ascend carefully for fear of tripping up. But all the care in the world could not prevent the ancient wood of the treads from creaking abominably, and each step he took sounded to him in the acute silence like a pistol shot.

He reached the top at last, however, and now that he was there the darkness that had looked so intense was less formidable. A little of the light from the window below managed to reach to the landing. Looking about him he discovered that to his right and to his left ran a passage, and the vague whispering seemed to come from the left-hand one. He started to feel his way towards the dark opening, and had taken half a dozen steps in its direction when a slight creaking from the hall below, made him stop dead, and at the same instant he realised that it was getting darker.

Hartley swung round and peered down the stairs. What he saw made the hair on the back of his neck tingle, and in spite of his iron nerves, he felt himself grow suddenly cold. The front door by which he had entered was slowly closing, and, even as he looked, it shut completely with a loud click. The darkness was now almost complete, and Hartley's first impulse was to produce his torch but for the second time that night prudence won. If, like a fool, he had walked into a trap and there were people unseen lurking in the blackness all a light would do would be to give himself away. He was safer in the dark, and, at any rate, on equal terms with his unknown adversaries. Crouching back against the wall, he listened. But no fresh sound reached his ears. The whispering had continued unchecked, but that was all. Apart from that, there was silence — a silence as complete as the darkness. What, then, had shut the door? Was it a material agency or — something else? Briggs had hinted that the place was reputed to be haunted. Certainly, after that faint creak and click, nothing had moved below.

Hartley waited motionless and several minutes passed, but nothing happened, and slightly reassured, he began to consider a further exploration. Perhaps, after all, it was the wind that had closed that door. Certainly there had been no wind when he came in, but it didn't take long for a breeze to spring up at night. Probably there was a broken window at the back somewhere, and the draught had swung to the door. Convincing himself that this was the explanation in spite of certain vague doubts that reason hinted. Hartley tiptoed cautiously along the left-hand passage, feeling his way by the wall. A little way along it turned abruptly to the right, and, at the far end he caught sight of a thin pencil of light shining beneath a closed door.

So the Moat Farm wasn't empty, after all! It had tenants, lawful or otherwise. Dr. Hartley was inclined to think otherwise, and started to creep towards that faint illumination with a thrill of expectancy. He was less than a yard away from it when a sound behind him brought him to a halt — the soft shuffle of feet! He turned in an instant, and the shuffling sound ceased. Not a sound but the increased murmur of voices from behind the closed door under which shone the light. And yet he couldn't have been mistaken. Somewhere in the darkness, the way he had come, someone or something lurked. He could sense their watchfulness could almost believe he saw the glimmer of eyes!

He could neither go forward, nor go back, and, suddenly making up his mind that at all costs he would see what it was that lurked in the passage he pulled his torch from his pocket and holding it out sideways at arm's length he switched it on. As the rays stabbed the blackness there was a rush of feet, and for an instant before the lamp was knocked from his hand he found himself staring into a shining yellow face of inconceivable malignity — the face of a Chinaman!

Hartley hit at it blindly, and felt his wrist caught in a grip of steel. A hand fastened on his throat, and he strove with all his force to wrench away the clinging fingers. There was a shout, and a door banged open behind him, letting out a stream of light. He kicked out, and his foot hit something solid. There was a grunt of pain, and the grip on this throat tightened savagely. He heard a confused babel of voices, and the sharp crack of a pistol, and noticed that the passage seemed to have become full of struggling figures. There came a roaring in his ears, and a blood-red mist seemed to float before his eyes.

With a last desperate attempt to break away, he smashed his bunched fist with all his force at that snarling, twisted yellow face. The grip on his throat relaxed, and with great panting gasps he gulped down the air into his tortured lungs, and then something crashed on to his head, and all the darkness in the world engulfed him in a flood!

8

The Other Prisoner

A sound like the gentle trickle of running water heralded Dr. Hartley's return to consciousness from that enveloping mantle of blackness. For some time in an intermediate state between waking and dreaming, he listened and pictured himself lying by the side of a river on a hot day, with the bees humming in the distance, and the sun hot on his head. Heavens, how hot that sun was! It seemed to be burning into his brain. He tried to raise a hand to his forehead, but found himself powerless to move.

Presently the dream faded to reality as his senses overcame his physical incapability, and he opened his eyes. A faint light flickered on a table, and he discovered that he was lying in a large, low-ceilinged room lighted by a single candle. The sound of trickling water and the humming of bees resolved itself into a monotonous, chanting voice, and the hot sun became a very real and acute pain in his head, and then he remembered!

The malignant yellow face, the shots and the sound of excited voices, that strangle-hold on his throat, and the sudden stunning blow —

He looked about him, and the sight that met his cautious gaze was one that even in his wildest imaginings he could never have dreamed.

The low-ceilinged room was bare, and empty of furniture save for a dilapidated chair and the table on which stood the candle. The floor on which he lay was inches thick in grey dust, and the raftered ceiling black with age and ancient grime, but it was neither the room nor the shooting pain in his head that caused him to catch his breath with sharp intake. It was the picture presented by the occupants of that long-disused apartment. There were four. One white man and three Chinamen. Two of the Chinamen stood impassively by the closed door, looking oddly out of place in their

European clothes. The third — a tall, commanding figure — stood by the table, surveying the Englishman, who, securely bound hand and foot, had been propped up against the wall by the window, his white, strained face streaked with dirt and blood.

The tall Chinaman — and never in his life had Hartley seen such a cruel, inhuman mask for a face — was speaking slowly and distinctly in almost perfect English, but with the slight sibilant accent of his race.

'Once again I should advise you to divulge the whereabouts of the Sacred Idol,' he purred softly, but with a world of menace in his voice. 'We have — er — methods which can be guaranteed to make the most obstinate people speak, and I assure that I shall not hesitate to use them should it become necessary.'

'I've told you, you yellow devil!' burst forth the man by the window. 'I know nothing about your confounded idol!'

'You have probably in your life told many such lies,' said the Chinaman gravely, 'and that this is a lie I am well aware. You were seen by Loo Ki to take the image from the cabin of the Englishman Mallory — curses be on both him and his ancestors — after you had killed the steward who discovered you. But for the hue-and-cry that was raised, Loo Ki would have secured it from you on the ship. As it was, he waited, hoping to get it when you disembarked at the London Docks. Unfortunately for Loo Ki' — the level, droning voice paused — 'he lost track of you. For that error he has paid. Others, however, were more successful. Aided by the description Loo Ki was able to give before he slept upon the Terrace of the Night, you were traced to the village of Hailsham. I suggest that, in order to avoid further unpleasantness, you tell me where the idol is.'

'I'll see you in Hades first!' snarled the man who had spoken before, and Dr. Hartley recognised him now as one of his and Jack Mallory's fellow-passengers — a silent, dark-faced man named Silverton, who had spent most of the voyage reading and drinking in the smoke-room. 'Since you appear to know so much, you can find out the rest!'

'I intend to,' purred the tall Chinaman. 'You have much to answer for. Your hands have defiled the Sacred Image.' He bowed slightly every time he mentioned the idol. 'And to-night you have in cold blood taken the life of Ho Ling. Such things must not go unpunished.'

Silverton gave a harsh laugh.

'Ho Ling only got his deserts!' he sneered. 'His hands were wet with the blood of an old man whom he'd just murdered. It was only justice that he should die.'

The thin figure by the table drew itself up to its full height.

'Who are you that you should speak of justice,' he asked menacingly, 'you who do not even know the meaning of honour! Is it not justice that those who pillage the sacred relics of the temples for the lust of wealth should suffer? The old man to whom you refer would not have been killed if he had kept his covetous hands off things which were not his. He took, by the aid of bribery, things which were China's and had been China's for generation upon generation — the manuscripts of Tsao-Sun!'

As if a shaft of light had suddenly been focused on a dark picture, Hartley saw the coherent shape of the puzzle that had been bothering him before his eyes.

So that was the reason for the death of Arlington! That was why he had been returning on the same ship that carried the son of his future neighbour. While Jack Mallory's trip to China had been made for the purpose of stealing the Black Idol, Arlington's, by one of those curious coincidences that are more common in fact than in fiction, had been for the purpose of gaining possession of the manuscripts of Tsao-Sun — the very manuscripts that Jack had spoken of in describing how the idol could be opened.

So, thought Dr. Hartley, his suspicion that Arlington had stolen the image from Jack's cabin had been wrong. In all probability the professor hadn't even known it was on board, for even after the tragedy the fact that anything had been stolen at all had only been known to the captain, Jack Mallory, the purser, and Hartley himself, and, with the exception of the Chinese in the steerage, the passengers' luggage had not been searched. Hartley's thoughts were abruptly switched back to the scene before him, for the tall Chinaman was speaking again.

'Those manuscripts originally stolen and sold to Professor Arlington by a treacherous dog of a half-caste who has since suffered the death of a Thousand Cuts for his infamy,' he continued, 'were recovered to-night by Ho Ling. On his way to meet me with them he was killed and robbed by you. The idol was useless to you without the knowledge of how to gain access to the jewels, for it was the jewels you wanted. You thought the manuscripts were in the possession of the Englishman Mallory, for I have heard that twice you tried to break into his home. You were gloating over your prize when I and my servants took you unawares in spite of your spy whom you had left on guard outside the door.'

He turned and glanced at Hartley through the almond slits of his eyes.

'You're wrong for once,' snarled Silverton, 'if you think that fellow in the passage was a spy of mine. He's a friend of the Englishman Mallory, as you call him, and his name's Dr. Hartley.'

'So!' breathed the tall Chinaman softly, and his oblique eyes regarded the doctor more intently. He tapped the table gently with his long fingers. 'Whether or not he was a spy of yours is immaterial. What I am anxious for at the moment is to learn the whereabouts of the Black Buddha of Tsao-Sun.'

'Well, you can find out yourself!' said Silverton. 'I shan't tell you!'

'I think you will,' retorted the other smoothly. 'I am sure you will — after a little persuasion.'

'What do you mean?' A momentary flicker of fear flashed in Silverton's eyes at the intonation the Chinaman had given to the last four words.

'You will see — and feel — what I mean,' came the sibilant reply, and one long ivory hand signed to the two motionless figures by the door. 'It was lucky for your friend — the third man who was here — that he got away!'

In silence — a silence that was more impressive than any speech — they stepped swiftly forward, and picking up Silverton as though he had been a child of six, carried him over and laid him on his back across the table. It creaked protestingly under his struggles and the impassive figure standing watching picked up the candle and held it while the other two swiftly and methodically bound their victim in position.

'Gag him!' ordered the tall Chinaman in the same level, emotionless voice he had used throughout. 'If he changes his mind later — as he will do — he can nod his head. In the meanwhile, since the little operation that I propose to inflict is likely to lead to a vocal demonstration it will be better if he is effectually silenced.'

Dr. Hartley watched fascinated, a cold feeling in the region of his spine. He had both read of and experienced something of the Chinese methods of persuasion, and was prepared for anything. In spite of the fact that the man Silverton was undoubtedly a murderer and a thief, he would have gone to his assistance if he had been free. But neither the cords at his wrists and ankles nor the gag round his mouth shifted the fraction of an inch for all his endeavours.

'I'm afraid that of necessity we shall have to be rather crude in our methods,' went on the Chinaman smoothly. 'But although severely handicapped by lack of the proper implements to carry out the more subtle forms of torture for which my country is noted, I think we can improvise something that will have the desired effect. Take off his right shoe and sock.'

With the same unhurried precision that had marked the carrying out of his other orders, this was done.

'Now,' hissed the level voice, 'before we start the next stage, for the last time where is the Black Buddha? Nod your head if you are prepared to tell me and save — unpleasantness.'

Silverton remained motionless. Only his eyes, wide and staring, glared defiance at his questioner, and whatever the man's character might be, Dr. Hartley couldn't help feeling admiration at his undoubted pluck.

'So!' It was more of a breath than a word. 'Very well.' He extended the candle in his thin, ivory clawlike hand and one of the other Chinamen took it from him with a grin distorting his pock-marked yellow face. 'Hold the flame under the naked sole of his foot!'

The grinning celestial obeyed with obvious delight, and as the flame impinged upon the flesh Silverton jerked his foot back as far as the cords would let him, spasmodically. The candle was held there, its flame playing against the sole of his foot; but although his eyes twitched with the pain he didn't give in. For perhaps five seconds the flame scorched his flesh, and then at a sign from the tall Chinaman it was removed.

'Are you prepared to speak?' he asked, and Silverton shook his head. 'You are obstinate my friend,' hissed the other. 'But I can be patient, knowing that eventually you will give me the information that I desire.' He made a gesture, and once more the flame of the candle flickered against the bare flesh. 'This time it will remain there until you decide to alter your mind.'

The seconds passed slowly and no sign came from the man across the table, although his agony must have been intense. Hartley felt the perspiration streaming down his own face and his blood boiled at the callousness of the Chinaman who stood watching with expressionless face for his victim's nerve to break under the pain of the slowly roasting flesh.

At last it did. Silverton's tensed muscles relaxed and a groan burst from his lips half-choked by the gag.

'You are ready to speak?' asked his torturer quickly, and across his immobile face flickered a quick flash of satisfaction.

Silverton nodded and instantly the gag was removed from his mouth.

'You inhuman devil!' he gasped, hoarse with the agony he had endured. 'You yellow brute!'

The other took not the slightest notice of his abuse.

'Where is the Sacred Image?' he breathed.

'Over there — hidden in the chimney,' muttered Silverton and burst into a string of profanity.

With swift, cat-like steps, the tall Chinaman went over to the rubbish-heaped grate and, bending down, felt about in the narrow opening of the old-fashioned flue. Presently with a little exclamation in his own tongue, he extricated a heavy object with difficulty and bore it tenderly and reverently over to the table. It was the Black Idol, almost unrecognisable now owing to its covering of soot and crumbling mortar.

'Oh, Lord of Cathay,' cried the Chinaman bowing low before it. 'Buddha has smiled upon me, Li-Sin, and upon my ancestors, and my children shall be blessed, for it is decreed that my unworthy hands shall restore the Sacred Image to the Temple of Tsao-Sun.'

'That sounds very nice indeed,' snapped a youthful voice from the door, 'but in the meanwhile I should advise you to put your unworthy hands above your head and keep still. I think the police will shortly be wanting a word with all of you!'

Dr. Hartley twisted round and saw Eric standing in the doorway, an automatic in his hand covering the group by the table. He only saw him for a second and then the candle went out and the whole room was plunged in darkness!

9

The Crook Wins

Crack!

Crack! Crack!

The whip-like reports of an automatic shattered the sudden silence which fell as the candle was extinguished, and Hartley saw the vicious orange spears of flame stab the blackness from the direction of the door. A shrill squeal of pain followed the last shot, and almost instantly pandemonium broke out. There was a shuffling of feet, the sound of heavy breathing and the dull smack of flesh against flesh.

There came a clattering thud as something fell to the floor and he heard Eric's voice shouting hoarsely above the hubbub. There was an answering call from below which he recognised as emanating from Sir Edward and the stairs creaked loudly. Feet were trampling all round him, and once a pair of struggling figures tripped over his legs and fell crashing to the floor. Once or twice there came a grunt from Eric and a muttered curse from Sir Edward who had apparently joined in the mêlée, and occasionally a little high-pitched twittering in the bird-like dialect of China, but for the most part that fight in the dark was carried on in silence.

And it ended as abruptly as it had begun. Two tremendous crashes shook the room and instantly afterwards there was a scurrying of feet, followed by the banging of the door and the sound of hurried retreating steps along the passage.

'Don't let them get away!' panted Eric's voice, and Hartley heard the lad stumble across the room in pursuit.

A door crashed to below, and presently somewhere outside came the low hum of a car engine being started. At the same instant somebody shouted and there came a fusillade of shots. Eric's voice reached Hartley's ears, talking excitedly, and then the car engine revved up to a roar and began to fade away in the distance. There was the sound of a match being struck and a pale glimmer broke the darkness. Sir Edward was sitting on the floor holding a lighted match in his hand and looking dazedly about him. He caught sight of the candle that had rolled under the table, and retrieving it, lighted the wick carefully.

As the stronger illumination put to flight the shadows, Hartley saw that, though Silverton still remained strapped to the table, the Black Idol had disappeared.

Sir Edward set the candle down on the table gingerly and then came over and inspected Hartley. As he recognised who it was, his mouth opened in an O of surprise.

'Hartley, by Jove!' he ejaculated, and bending down, proceeded to untie the gag from the doctor's mouth. He had only just succeeded in loosing the knot when they heard voices and footsteps on the stairs, and Eric entered followed by Jack Mallory.

'Good Heavens!' gasped Sir Edward, looking round. 'Where did you get that?'

And Dr. Hartley freed of the gag, followed the direction of his gaze.

Jack was holding in his arms the Black Idol!

'I arrived in time to see three Chinese making off with it in a car,' he explained, setting the sinister-looking image down on the floor. 'Two of them were already in the car and the other, a tall, thin fellow, was just getting in with that. I wrenched the thing out of his hands and he turned round like a wild beast and attacked me. Then Eric appeared on the scene, and he thought better of it eventually, and, jumping into the car, it made off. I fired several shots at the tail lamp hoping I'd get one of the tyres. I must have missed — anyway, it didn't stop.'

'It's a pity you didn't let them get away with the thing,' remarked Dr. Hartley grimly shaking himself free of the cords which Sir Edward had cut. 'It's been the cause of enough trouble already. But we left you looking after Miss Marsh. How did you get here?'

Jack explained that after the house-keeper had put the girl to bed he had waited for them to return, but when no one came back he had walked over to Haslemere. He had arrived to find a constable in charge and Briggs asleep in the drawing room. The butler had told him that Sir Edward and Eric had waited for some time for Hartley's return and had then set off for the Moat Farm in search of him as they had begun to get uneasy.

'That's right,' broke in the lad. 'I didn't like the guv'nor going alone in the first place. We apparently arrived just at the right time.'

'Well, I came over after you to see what was happening,' said Jack. 'Briggs couldn't tell me anything except a rambling story of a Chinaman having been found dead in some bushes. What has been happening here and how did that thing' — he jerked his head towards the squatting image — 'turn up again?'

Dr. Hartley explained briefly what had happened and what he had learnt.

'So it was this fellow who did in the poor devil of a steward, was it?' muttered Jack glancing at Silverton. 'Well, anyway, you've got something to show for your night's work.'

'Yes,' answered the doctor, 'and before we go any further I think the best thing we can do will be to turn him over to Inspector Parrish.'

'What are you going to do with the idol?' asked Sir Edward, and Hartley frowned.

'I suppose it had better go back to your place,' he said. 'Frankly I wish those Chinese had got away with it. Strictly speaking, it's their property and though I am by no means in sympathy with their methods, I should feel greatly relieved if it was out of our possession. I'm afraid there will be nothing but trouble until it's once more back in the place where it belongs. They're hardly likely to let things rest as they are. They know that Jack's got the idol now, and before very long they'll be planning steps to gain possession of it. However' — he walked over to the table and looked down at Silverton who returned his gaze with a glare of fury — 'we can discuss all that later. In the meanwhile let's cut this fellow free and get away from here as soon as possible.'

Hartley took the knife that Sir Edward had used to cut his own bonds, and slashed through the cords securing Silverton to the table. As the man rose and rubbed his cramped limbs he was revealed as about the average height, but broad-shouldered and deep-chested so that he looked less tall than he really was.

'Put on your shoe and sock,' ordered the doctor after he had run his hands over the other's pockets and assured himself that he had no weapon on him.

Silverton obeyed sullenly binding the burn on his foot first, with his handkerchief.

'Now, then,' said Hartley when the man was ready, turning to Jack, 'if you'll take the Black Idol, Mallory, over to the Hall, Eric and I will escort this fellow into Hailsham and see him safely locked up in the police-station under the care of Inspector Parrish.'

The man was not armed and there were three to one, so that there was an excuse for Hartley's momentary lack of vigilance, but it was to prove his undoing. He had forgotten one thing which ever since he had been released Silverton had spotted and awaited his opportunity — Eric's automatic which had been knocked from the lad's hand by the tall Chinaman when the candle had gone out, and which now lay over by the wall.

When Hartley turned to address Jack, Silverton gathered himself together and, as the doctor finished his sentence, bounded forward and picked up the weapon. Eric's warning shout came too late. Before any of them could move, the crook was crouching by the door; the wicked black muzzle of the automatic covering them.

'Put up your hands, all of you,' he snarled his lips drawn back in a mirthless grin. 'The first one of you who moves will never move again!'

His deep-set eyes shifted from one to the other.

'Thought you'd get me didn't you?' he rasped hoarsely. 'But you haven't — yet. It's a hanging job if I'm caught, so I might as well hang for four as for one. Besides, I want that idol. I've been to enough trouble to get it, and I mean to keep it if I can.'

'Don't be foolish, Silverton,' snapped Dr. Hartley sharply. 'You can't hold us up like this for ever.'

The other laughed harshly.

'I don't intend to,' he retorted. 'There's a cellar downstairs with a fairly solid door — about the only thing solid about this ramshackle hole — and you'll be safe enough there until I've got away.' He looked at Eric. 'Come here,' he said.

The lad hesitated and shrugging his shoulders, stepped forward. Silverton grabbed him by the arm and forced the muzzle of the automatic into the back of his neck.

'Now we're all nice and comfy,' he said looking at the others. 'You see the idea? If any of you tries any funny business I'll shoot this youngster.'

Dr. Hartley compressed his lips. They were helpless and he knew it. The slightest attempt to turn the tables would cause Silverton's finger to press the trigger. The man could, as he had said, only be hanged once, and by his daring move had got them in a cleft stick.

Hartley cursed himself for having over-looked that automatic lying on the floor. Silverton chuckled as he saw, by the doctor's face, that he had won.

'Now we'll get on without wasting any more time,' he said. 'You' — he nodded his head at Sir Edward — 'take the candle and lead the way downstairs and remember no hanky-panky. If you try any, this lad dies, and don't get the idea that I'm bluffing, because I'm not.'

In silence Sir Edward picked up the candle.

'You follow him,' ordered Silverton looking at Jack, 'and then you. I'll bring up the rear with this fellow.'

In the order he had indicated, they made their way along the passage and down the stairs.

'Turn to the right,' snapped the crook when they reached the hall. 'You'll find a door under the staircase.'

They found the door, a stout affair of oak secured by a bar and a padlock.

'The key's in the padlock,' Silverton went on. 'I left it there. Unlock it and give me both the padlock and the key.'

Hartley felt his blood boiling with fury

118

at the audacity of the man calmly ordering him to unlock his own prison, but for Eric's sake he had to swallow his anger and obey.

'There's a flight of stone steps leading downwards,' the man continued, when the key and the padlock had been placed in his hand. 'Go down to the bottom.'

The place was damp and musty and smelt of mildew and decay as Hartley followed Sir Edward and Jack down the worn steps.

'I hope somebody finds you soon,' chuckled Silverton. 'It's an unpleasant place to stay in long and overrun with rats.'

For a second he grinned down at their furious faces, and then, suddenly releasing his grip on Eric's collar, he gave the lad a push that sent him staggering down the steps and slammed the door shut. They heard the clang of the bar as it was rammed into place and the snap of the padlock. A mocking laugh, muffled by the heavy timber, floated down to their ears, and then the sound of retreating footsteps.

10

Rescued

Almost before the door barring the exit to the malodorous cellar had been shut and fastened Dr. Hartley was at the top of the steps. With all his force he hurled himself against the stout oak planks, but although the door creaked and groaned under the assault, the stout bar and the padlock held. Three times he tried but without result, and with nothing to show for his efforts except a bruised and aching shoulder, he rejoined the others.

'Nothing short of a battering ram will open that,' he said, and, seating himself on the lower step, philosophically lighted a cigarette.

Eric examined an ugly abrasion on his left leg, the result of his fall down the stone steps.

'Surely all three of us could break it open,' he suggested, but Hartley shook his head.

'I doubt it,' he replied. 'Apart from the central bar and padlock, there was a heavy bolt top and bottom and he's slipped them both. The house is an old one, and when it was built they built solidly.'

'Then what are we going to do?' asked Sir Edward in dismay.

'Stay here until somebody lets us out,' replied the doctor calmly.

'But nobody ever comes here,' said Jack, 'and if we shouted our heads off they wouldn't hear us from the road.'

'No, but they know where we went to at Haslemere,' said Hartley. 'Briggs knows — I asked him the way. And he also knows that you came here, too. When he finds that neither of us have come back, he'll either come to look for us or report the matter to the police. In either case it shouldn't be many hours before we're released.'

'In the meantime,' exploded Sir Edward angrily, 'that scoundrel will get clean away.'

Dr. Hartley shrugged his shoulders.

'It can't be helped,' he answered, 'though I admit it's annoying. However, so far as you and Jack are concerned, I'd rather the idol was in his keeping than in yours, and I should feel happier still if our Chinese friends knew that Silverton had got it, though I don't suppose it will take them long to find out.'

He stopped and held up his hand as the dull thud of a closing door boomed faintly above.

'That's Silverton departing,' he said. 'Now all we can do is to possess our souls in patience and wait until somebody comes and lets us out.'

Sir Edward stuck the candle on a ledge and looked about him. The cellar was filthy dirty with the accumulated debris of years, the stone-flagged floor inches deep in muddy slime. Over against one wall stood a pile of barrels. Most of them were staved in, but he and Jack managed to find two that were sufficiently strong to support their weights, and upon these they seated themselves, Eric and Hartley preferring the steps. Sir Edward lighted a cigar, and the fragrant tobacco overcame the musty smell of the place and rendered the air a little more breatheable.

Dr. Hartley looked at his watch and discovered that it was nearly two o'clock. How long would it be, he wondered, before the butler at Haslemere began to get alarmed at their absence and started to search for them. Perhaps he would go to bed in the belief that they had gone back to Mallory Hall, and in that case the morning would be well-advanced before they could hope to be released. One thing the doctor definitely decided there and then. So far as he was concerned he had finished with the whole matter. The Chinaman Ho Ling, who had killed Arlington was dead. Silverton had got the idol. Far better to let it go at that and finish his holiday with the Mallorys in peace. It was no concern of his now that his friends were not involved. Let Silverton and the police and the Chinese emissaries from the Temple of Tsao-Sun fight it out between them. He would place what information he had got in the hands of Inspector Parrish, and that worthy official could do the rest.

His strenuous evening had made him tired, and in the midst of his thoughts he fell into a doze. How long it lasted he couldn't tell, but he awoke feeling icy cold and cramped. The candle had burned down to the merest rind. Sir Edward was leaning back against the wall, his arms folded on his chest snoring gutturally.

'What time is it?' whispered Jack who was awake, as Hartley rose to his feet and stretched himself. 'I forgot to wind my watch, and it's stopped.'

The doctor glanced at his own.

'Half-past three,' he said, and Eric groaned.

'Gosh, is that all, guv'nor?' he grunted. 'I thought we'd been here for hours.'

'It's extraordinary how slowly time passes when you want it to go quickly,' began Jack, searching in his pocket for his cigarette case. 'Well, I suppose — ' He broke off, the open case in his hand, and listened. 'I thought I heard voices!' he exclaimed.

In the silence that followed, they strained their ears, but there was no sound.

'You must have made a mistake,' said

Eric, but even as he spoke he heard a muffled call.

'There you are!' cried Jack excitedly. 'That was somebody shouting. Thank heaven they've found us.'

There was a heavy tramping above, and now Dr. Hartley, who had mounted to the top of the stone steps and was listening at the door, heard a voice call distinctly:

'Hallo!' it cried. 'Is there anybody here?'

'Yes!' shouted the doctor in answer. 'We're here — in the cellar.'

The tramping of feet stopped and then a single pair of footsteps approached the cellar door.

'Who called?' demanded a voice that, muffled as it was, Hartley recognised as belonging to Inspector Parrish.

'I did — Hartley!' roared the doctor. 'Open the door — we're locked in.'

Inspector Parrish uttered a forceful ejaculation, and there came the rattle of the padlock.

'There's no key here,' he bawled disgustedly. 'Can you tell me where it is?'

'Never mind the key,' replied Hartley impatiently. 'Get hold of something and smash the hoop.'

'All right!'

The rattling ceased and the heavy feet of the inspector walked away. For what seemed an interminable time nothing further happened and then the footsteps returned.

'I've found an iron bar in one of the outhouses,' shouted the inspector triumphantly. 'We'll have you out in a jiffy now.'

There was a slight pause, and then a rasping of metal against metal, followed by much panting, and then a loud crack.

'Done it!' cried Parrish exultantly, and a few seconds later Hartley had the satisfaction of seeing the door of their prison pulled open.

The noise had aroused Sir Edward, and presently they found themselves standing shivering in the gloomy hall of the Moat Farm.

Inspector Parrish was accompanied by two stalwart farm-labourers and Briggs, who stared open-mouthed as they emerged from the cellar.

'How did you manage to get yourselves locked up there?' demanded the inspector, scratching his head.

'We didn't get ourselves locked up,' snapped Dr. Hartley. 'We were locked in by a man called Silverton.'

He briefly related to the surprised and wondering inspector the adventures of the evening, and that worthy listened, accompanying Hartley's narrative with grunts, and a considerable amount of head-scratching.

'By Gosh!' he ejaculated, when the doctor had finished. 'Whoever would have thought it? In Hailsham of all places! Why, it sounds like one of those stories yer read!'

'It felt like it too,' retorted Dr. Hartley grimly, tenderly touching his still aching head.

'I got worried, sir,' put in Briggs, 'when you hadn't come back by two o'clock, and sent the second footman over to the 'All to see if you'd gone back there. When he reported you hadn't, I thought it was best to send post-haste for the inspector.'

'It's a jolly good thing you did, Briggs,'

said Sir Edward heartily. 'Now for heaven's sake let's get back to the Hall. I'm as cold as an icicle, and infernally tired.'

'I should like you to give me a description of this man Silverton and the Chinks, sir,' began Inspector Parrish, 'and I'll send out an all-stations call at once. They won't get far.'

Dr. Hartley gave him as graphic a description as he could.

'You'll probably find his finger-prints all over the place upstairs,' he said. 'I should have them photographed and sent to Scotland Yard. They may know him in the Records Department.'

Inspector Parrish agreed to this suggestion, and they left him nosing about the house with one of the labourers and a large electric lantern.

'And that's that,' remarked the doctor, as half-an-hour later they walked up the drive of Mallory Hall. 'Let us hope that nothing else will happen to disturb the peace of our holiday.'

The hope was destined to be unfulfilled, as he very shortly discovered.

Sir Edward suggested a drink before

going to bed, a suggestion with which Hartley hastily agreed as he was chilled to the bone, and they went into the library. The old butler, who had waited up for their return, anxiously after the visit of the footman from Haslemere, inquired if there was anything else.

'No thanks, Rowson,' said Sir Edward, busy at the sideboard, and the old man said goodnight and was turning away when Jack stopped him.

'How is Miss Marsh?' he asked.

Rowson looked at him, a puzzled expression on his face.

'Miss Marsh, sir?' he said. 'Didn't you see her, sir?'

'See her?' Jack frowned as he repeated the sentence. 'What do you mean? I left her asleep in the care of Mrs. Henderson.'

'I know, sir!' Rowson looked perplexed. 'But after you'd gone to Haslemere sir — some time after — a foreign gentleman called and said would Miss Marsh dress herself and go at once to her uncle's house. He said the police wanted to ask her some questions.'

Hartley's face suddenly went tense.

'Did she go?' he snapped.

'Yes, sir, she got dressed at once and went off with the gentleman, sir. He had a car waiting.'

'And what was this gentleman like?' asked Hartley, although he knew the answer.

'He was very tall and thin,' replied Rowson, 'and although he spoke good English, sir, he looked like a Chinaman!'

'Good Heavens!' The exclamation burst from Jack, and his face was pale and drawn. 'Hartley, it was that devil I saw getting into the car at the Moat Farm! What did he come here for? What does he want with Jill?'

Dr. Hartley didn't answer. He knew why the tall Chinaman had called at Mallory Hall and tricked the girl into going away with him. He was under the impression that they had got the Black Idol, and he was holding Jill Marsh as a hostage against its return.

11

The Idea of Li-sin

Jill Marsh had no misgivings when the message was brought to her that a gentleman had called to take her to Haslemere as she was wanted to answer some questions. Except for feeling a little sick and dizzy, she had quite recovered from her faint and the shock of finding her uncle dead across his desk. Dressing herself quickly she went down the stairs and was greeted by a profound bow from the tall stranger who was waiting in the hall. She was rather surprised when she saw he was a Chinaman, and he must have noticed this, for he hastened to explain his presence.

'I arrived, Miss Marsh,' he said smoothly, 'to keep an appointment with your uncle, and was surprised and grieved to learn of the tragedy that had occurred. The police who were busy investigating the crime wished for your presence and as it was very late I volunteered to drive round and fetch you.'

'It was very good of you,' she said and he bowed again.

'If you are quite ready,' he murmured apologetically, 'perhaps we had better be going. The matter was, I believe, rather urgent.'

She nodded and he led the way down the short flight of steps to a waiting car. Opening the door the tall Chinaman waited for her to get in, and then took his place beside her. She heard the engine spring to a swifter hum, and saw through the window Rowson closing the front door of Mallory Hall then something was jabbed sharply into her arm, she felt everything spin around her and lost consciousness.

It was a long time before Jill opened her eyes. A racking pain was crawling to life in her nerves and her head throbbed monotonously. She could feel every heartbeat repeated in her temples ten thousandfold. Her skin was hot and clammy and there was a feverish heat in her flesh that seemed to be burning her up. She was lying on something soft, but when she tried to get up the effort was beyond her. Her muscles refused to obey the signal from her brain. There seemed to be a dead insulation between herself and her senses. She tried to think but her mind refused to concentrate. It was as if she were dreaming yet knew herself to be awake. Somewhere above her a blaze of light was burning. It stabbed at her eyes and hurt them, cut into her head like knives and gave her a feeling of nausea. It was as though she were being revolved rapidly inside a spinning drum with no chance of either stopping the spinning or getting out. She closed her eyes and allowed herself to relax. For many minutes she lay, slipping back again into a state of comatose lethargy. She wasn't conscious of it, but she was experiencing all the misery and deadening lifelessness of the slow return from the drug with which her system had been charged.

Gradually she opened her eyes again. The light still blazed white-hot above her, but now it didn't seem to be so strong

— at any rate it didn't burn her eyes as it had done before. Vaguely she began to remember fleeting fragments of the events of the night, and tried to disentangle them from the patches of vacancy that surrounded them. Little flashing pictures of her uncle lying across the desk with the blood-marked papers strewn around him — of Jack springing forward to catch her — of the housekeeper smoothing her pillow — and between all these the vision of a tall, thin form with a yellow inscrutable face.

She felt angry with herself because she could remember nothing connected from this jumbled mass of glimpses, and then in the midst of her anger she drifted away on a sea of blackness once more.

When she woke again she woke to full consciousness and, like a flood, memory returned closely and sharply. With a violent effort of will she sat up, clenching her teeth as the movement made her head swim dizzily, and let her eyes wander vaguely about her. She was lying amid a heap of silken cushions on a low divan in the middle of a large room, completely empty save for the divan and two little inlaid stools.

Above her head from the centre of the draped ceiling hung an ornate silver lamp that shed a circle of light on the divan but left the rest of the room in shadow. She was able to see, however, that the walls were covered with beautifully-worked silk hangings and so far as she could make out there was no door. A rich heavily piled black-and-yellow carpet covered the floor, and warmth was provided by an electric radiator of the same precious metal as the lamp, carved to represent a peacock with spreading tail.

Jill rose unsteadily to her feet and gazed about this extraordinary room in bewilderment. Where was she and why had she been brought here? She looked at her wrist for the watch she always wore there, but remembered that in her hurry she had forgotten to put it on. She wondered if it was still night, but there seemed no means of finding out, for apparently the room contained no windows. The whole place was overpoweringly hot, and the air was filled with a vague, rather sickly perfume. Her throat felt dry and rough, and at that moment she would have given her soul for a cup of tea. Tea! By a correlation of ideas the thought sent her mind to the tall Chinaman who had called to fetch her from Mallory Hall. She remembered getting into the car and the sudden sharp pain in her arm. Evidently she had been drugged, but why?

Finding no satisfactory answer to this question she began to explore the room, lifting the hangings and trying to find some sort of a door. But there was none. The walls behind the silk were of panelled oak and appeared solid and unbroken.

She went back to the divan and sat down, to think, and she had barely seated herself when the feeling that she was being watched made her turn her head sharply.

Behind her stood the tall Chinaman!

There must have been some secret means of entering that room, but she had heard no sound.

He bowed as she looked at him, and then advanced a few steps towards her.

'You need have no fear,' he said softly

as she shrank away, 'No harm will come to you — yet.'

'Why have you brought me here?' she asked.

'I have brought you here,' he replied, 'in order to prove the truth of an old saying that 'Exchange is no robbery.' '

She looked her surprise, and he continued after a pause.

'There are friends of yours who have something that does not belong to them,' he said, 'something that I am most anxious to possess. I propose to keep you here until that something is handed over to me. When that has happened, you will be sent back to your friends.'

She frowned.

'Who are the friends you refer to?' she asked. 'And what is the something you want?'

'The friends,' he answered, 'are Sir Edward Mallory and his son. The something is the Sacred Idol of Tsao-Sun!' He made a little stiff bow as he spoke.

Jill shook her head.

'I don't know what you are talking about,' she said.

'It is immaterial,' he replied, looking at her without any expression at all on his immobile face. 'So long as you write the letter that I desire, that is all I ask of you.'

'Letter?' she stammered questioningly.

He nodded slowly.

'You will write to your friends at Mallory Hall,' he said, 'and tell them that you are safe and that you will remain unharmed so long as they agree to give up the Sacred Idol.' Again he made that stiff little bow. 'If it is placed in the hands of the messenger, who will be waiting to receive it at the junction of the Southampton and Hailsham roads the day after tomorrow at midnight, you will be returned to your home within two hours afterwards. If they refuse — ' for the first time he raised the heavy lids that partially obscured his eyes and she caught the glint of them — 'if they refuse, you can tell them that for every day after that time that the Sacred Idol remains in their possession you will lose one of your finger-nails. It is a painful process and I should not advise you to allow things to reach that stage.'

Jill Marsh suppressed a little cry of horror. The words were spoken quietly enough, but she knew that the tall figure before her meant everything he said.

'You wouldn't do it, you dare not do it!' she whispered.

Li-Sin smiled, a mirthless smile that showed his yellow, opium-stained teeth.

'I shouldn't be too sure of that,' he replied. 'Unless they agree to give up that which is China's, I shall carry out my threat. I have no desire to hurt you, but — '

He shrugged his thin shoulders, and in silence crossed to one of the low inlaid tables. Pulling open a drawer he took out paper, ink and a pen.

'I think,' he said, 'you had better do as I ask.'

12

The Threat

It was a melancholy party that sat down to lunch at Mallory Hall on the afternoon following the discovery of Jill Marsh's disappearance. Lack of sleep had rendered their faces drawn and haggard, for none of them had gone to bed since their return from Moat Farm. Immediately after hearing Rowson's story, Dr. Hartley had phoned through to the police station at Hailsham to try and get in touch with Inspector Parrish, but that official was not there, and it was not until nearly an hour later that the doctor was able to get hold of him.

He listened in dismay to the news, and promised to send out a hurry call, containing a description of Jill and the car, to all stations at once. There was a possible chance that this might have some effect, but Hartley felt dubious. Although it was an uncommon thing for a white girl to be in the company of three Chinese they had no very clear description of the car, besides which by the time the descriptions were broadcast the girl and her captors would probably have reached their destination.

Hartley felt helpless. To try to trace the car itself once it had left the drive of Mallory Hall, without the number to go on, was an impossible task. Three miles beyond the village the Hailsham road joined the main Southampton-London road, and a mile further on were four cross-roads, any one of which might have been the route taken by the kidnappers. There was nothing to do but to wait for further developments — if any.

Hartley felt pretty sure that the girl would be safe enough, for he was convinced that the object of the whole plot had been to provide the Chinese emissaries from Tsao-Sun with a basis for bargaining for the Black Idol. The thing that worried him most was that they had not got the image with which to effect an exchange should such a matter be suggested. Personally, the doctor would have been only too glad to hand it over to the people to whom it undoubtedly belonged and get shot of the whole trouble.

But Silverton had it. The question was, supposing Li-Sin demanded the Black Idol in exchange for Jill Marsh, what were they going to say to him? Would he for one moment believe that Silverton had got away with it again? Hartley felt fairly certain that he would not. He would not unnaturally assume that they were trying to trick him.

It was not surprising, therefore, that having reached these conclusions, Dr. Hartley should feel worried. Added to which, he had to do his best to pacify Jack, for the loss of the girl had driven that young gentleman almost frantic.

Lunch from a social point of view could not by any stretch of the imagination be called a success. Sir Edward ate in silence, a deep and permanent frown marring his usually smooth brow. Jack didn't eat at all, but smoked a perpetual string of cigarettes, and drank more wine than was good either for his liver or his temper. Only Eric did full justice to the meal, for it took a good deal to upset his appetite, however worried he might be.

They had coffee served in the library, and afterwards Jack announced his intention of going for a walk, and left them to their own devices. Sir Edward dropped off into a doze, a proceeding which Eric evidently considered a good idea, for a few seconds afterwards he followed his host's example. Dr. Hartley made a pretence of reading, but the book might as well have been written in Hebrew for all that he knew of the contents, and presently he gave up even that camouflage and resigned himself to his thoughts.

The interminable afternoon dragged itself to a close at last. Jack came back at tea-time, apparently none the better for his walk, and savagely munched a toasted scone in silence.

It was not until six o'clock that the letter arrived, the contents of which were to start Hartley off on a quest that at the outset seemed impossible. It was addressed to Sir Edward, and his startled exclamation as he glanced at the sheet of heavily-scented paper caused them to look at him expectantly.

'Good heavens!' he ejaculated hoarsely, 'this is dreadful!'

He tossed the letter over to Hartley, ignoring his son's question, and the doctor read:

'Dear Sir Edward,

I am writing this at the dictation of the man who abducted me from your house last night. I am unharmed at present but unless you can comply with his wishes, I am not likely to remain so long. He says that you have in your possession the Sacred Idol of Tsao-Sun, and if you are prepared to give this up, I shall be released at once. He is sending a messenger at twelve o'clock tomorrow night to the place where the Hailsham road joins the Southampton road. If you will give him the idol everything will be all right, and I shall be allowed to go free. If not, for every day after the time the messenger returns empty handed, I am to lose one of my finger-nails. I am sure he really means this, so please, Sir Edward, let him have what he wants.

'Yours sincerely,
'JILL MARSH.'

Dr. Hartley's face set sternly as he read, and Jack who was leaning over his shoulder went white to the lips.

'What can we do?' he asked. 'We must do something. We've got to get Jill out of that fiend's clutches.'

The doctor laid the letter down on the table and stared at it with half-closed eyes.

'There's only one thing to be done,' he answered after a moment's pause, 'and that is to find the Black Idol by twelve o'clock tomorrow night.'

Jack uttered an impatient exclamation.

'What's the good of talking like that?' he almost shouted. 'How can we find the thing? It's impossible.'

'It's the only way out,' said Hartley, and his jaw projected in what Eric called his fighting expression. 'We've got to get the

Black Idol back by midnight tomorrow and hand it over to the messenger who will be waiting at the junction of the roads.'

'Surely there's some other way?' protested Sir Edward. 'Besides, even supposing that we could find the image by then, what proof have we that this scoundrel will keep his word and release Miss Marsh? Once he's got the idol he may murder her.'

Dr. Hartley shook his head.

'I don't think you need be afraid of that,' he said. 'These Chinese have got no quarrel with Miss Marsh. All they want is their property back.'

'By Heaven,' cried Jack, pacing up and down in his excitement. 'I wish I'd never seen the cursed thing!'

'It's too late to think about that now,' said Hartley sharply. 'All we can do is to try and prevent its causing any further trouble.' He looked at the clock on the mantelpiece. 'Six-fifteen. H'm! Can I keep awake for another twenty-nine and three-quarter hours?'

'What do you mean?' demanded Jack

146

coming to a sudden halt.

'This is going to be a race against time,' replied Dr. Hartley grimly. 'There's one way we can find the idol, and that's to find Silverton. The question is, can I find him in twenty-nine and three-quarter hours? If I can then the Black Idol can be returned to its rightful owners and Jill Marsh will be saved!'

13

A New Trail

Half an hour after the receipt of Jill
Marsh's letter, Dr. Hartley was on his
way to London. He arrived at Harley
Street shortly after eight o'clock and,
leaving Eric to await instructions went
straight on to Scotland Yard. He had
called on Inspector Parrish before leaving
Hailsham, and secured from that official
copies of the photographs Parrish had
taken of the finger-prints at Moat Farm,
and armed with these, he entered the
grim building on the Embankment and
asked for Detective-Inspector Gladwin,
his friend.

The Scotland Yard man was usually to
be found working late — in fact his
enemies said that he slept at the Yard, but
this was a gross libel — and to-night was
no exception.

Hartley discovered the burly inspector

seated behind his big desk, writing a report and Gladwin looked up with a grunt of pleasure as he entered.

'Hello, Dr. Hartley!' he greeted laying down his pen and running his stubby fingers through his close-cropped bristling hair. 'What brings you here, eh?'

The doctor seated himself in the chair facing his friend, and gave a brief but fairly detailed account of the task he had set himself.

Gladwin frowned when he had finished, and tugged at his toothbrush moustache.

'H'm!' he commented. 'I don't think you've got much chance of finding this fellow. It's like looking for a needle when you don't even know which haystack it's in. He may not even be in London.'

'I quite agree with you,' assented Hartley. 'At the same time I think London's the most likely place he'll have made for. The first thing, Gladwin, is have you any record of the man?'

He took the finger-print photographs from his pocket and handed them to the Scotland Yard man.

'These are his finger-prints,' he said. 'If he's an habitual criminal, Records should be able to tell us quite a lot about him.'

Gladwin glanced at the photograph and pressed a bell.

'It won't be difficult to find out,' he grunted. 'But even then I don't see how it's going to help you. Given time, of course, we should eventually pull him in, but you've only a little over twenty-four hours.'

He stopped as a uniformed constable entered in response to his summons.

'Take these along to Superintendent Singleton,' ordered Gladwin handing the man the photographs, 'and ask him to let me have a report on them at once.'

The constable saluted and when he had withdrawn the burly inspector continued his interrupted remarks.

'You see, doctor,' he said, playing with the pen on his blotting-pad, 'there's a murder charge against him if he's caught, and that's going to make him lie low. As long as he does that, it's next door to impossible to find him. If he was on the run — if he tried to leave the country, it would be a different matter, but he's probably too cute for that. He must know that, after that affair at Moat Farm, his description will have been circulated, and that the police will be looking for him, and that's going to make him extra careful.'

Dr. Hartley nodded.

'I see all the difficulties you mention,' he said, 'and a lot more that you haven't, but all the same the only way to save that girl is to find Silverton.'

'Personally,' remarked Gladwin, 'I should have thought it would have been easier to find the girl. Where was the letter posted?'

'E.C.4,' answered the doctor; 'but that doesn't tell us anything. It was probably posted in quite a different district from the one in which it was written. No, I think it would be a disastrous move to try and discover where they've got Miss Marsh. I've no doubt that both my movements and those of the Mallorys are being watched — the Chinese are a suspicious race — and any attempt to find their hiding-place would result in immediate action — probably the girl's death.'

Gladwin pursed his thick lips.

'Perhaps you're right, Dr. Hartley,' he agreed. 'I certainly see your point, but what I don't see is how you're going to get hold of Silverton even supposing we've got any record of him.'

Dr. Hartley shrugged his shoulders wearily.

'Neither do I,' he confessed, 'but I'm going to do my best.'

He drew out his cigar-case, and handed it to Gladwin. The inspector helped himself, and for a while they smoked in silence. Dr. Hartley was beginning to feel the effect of his sleepless night, but he fought off the drowsiness that threatened to overtake him. He knew that it was only while he was sitting still that he would feel that longing for sleep. Once there was a chance of action it would slip from him like a cloak and he would be his usual alert self.

The question was would there be any chance of action? Something had to be done but what? The hands of the clock were relentlessly creeping on — time was passing, and with every second that ticked away into infinity, the hour fixed for that appointment at the junction of the roads drew nearer.

Hartley knew enough of Chinese methods to feel sure that the threat contained in the letter would be carried out. They would have no qualms. Unless the Black Idol was forthcoming Jill Marsh would suffer. Dr. Hartley gave an involuntary shiver as his imagination pictured the scene, and it was just as well that at that moment the constable returned and switched his thoughts back to the business on hand.

'Superintendent Singleton sent this, sir,' said the messenger, laying a thin folder on the desk in front of Gladwin.

'All right.' The inspector nodded a dismissal. 'I'll ring when I want you to take 'em back.' He opened the folder and looked at the contents — several typewritten sheets and photographs. 'Well your man seems to have been through our hands all right,' he remarked, when the constable had gone. And then, as he turned over the papers he gave a sharp exclamation and whistled softly. 'By Jove!' he ejaculated. 'It's Henry Arthur Young!'

Dr. Hartley leaned forward, his grey eyes alight with interest. 'Henry Arthur Young!' he repeated softly. 'Isn't that the man who was convicted seven years ago for blackmail?'

Gladwin nodded.

'That's the fellow,' he grunted. 'Prior to that, he was sentenced to three years for obtaining money by false pretences.' He glanced rapidly over the typewritten official blanks containing the man's particulars, description, and list of previous convictions. 'He is apparently a pretty bad character and dangerous too,' he went on. 'The time he was arrested he injured severely one of the detectives who went to pull him in. He nearly always works alone, but is known to be friendly with a man called Levy, or the 'Slogger'.'

Hartley interrupted him by bringing the flat of his hand down on the desk with a bang.

'I know the Slogger,' he said. 'He keeps a public-house, the Pewter Pot, in Lower Water Lane, Deptford.'

'That's right,' agreed Gladwin. 'It's a filthy den, the meeting-place of all the riff-raff that infest the district. We've tried over and over again to get it closed up, but the Slogger's cunning — he keeps on the right side of the law — and although we're pretty sure he does a little fencing on the quiet we've never been able to get any proof.' He raised his eyebrows as Hartley rose to his feet. 'Are you going?' he said.

'Unless you can give me more information regarding Henry Arthur Young,' said the doctor.

'I can't,' answered the Scotland Yard man, 'and what I have given you won't help much I'm afraid.'

'It may and it may not,' said Hartley. 'Anyway it's given me a jumping-off place which I hadn't got before.' Gladwin looked dubious.

'If you're hoping to get any information out of the Slogger,' he growled. 'I think you'll be disappointed. One of his rules in life is never to know anything.'

'I'm not going to ask him anything,' retorted the doctor, 'but I feel that a visit

155

to the Pewter Pot may yield results.'

'You'd better be careful,' warned the burly inspector. 'It's a pestilential neighbourhood, and the Slogger's place is the worst spot in it.'

'I'll risk it,' said Dr. Hartley with a smile. 'I think I can take care of myself.' He glanced at his watch. 'Well, I'll be getting along. Thanks for the information.'

'You're welcome, doctor.' Gladwin gripped Hartley's extended hand. 'Though I'm not very hopeful that it's going to be of any use.'

'I can't say I'm very sanguine myself,' replied Dr. Hartley. 'But there's just a chance, a slender one, I know, but I'm going to take it.'

'Good luck,' said the Scotland Yard man gruffly, but he shook his head after the doctor had gone and for a long time stared at his blotting-pad before he picked up his pen and continued writing his report.

14

Down East

Lower Water Lane, Deptford, E., is narrow, dingy and remarkably dirty. If the houses of, say, Fitzroy Square were crowded into a breathless thoroughfare where it would be impossible for two taxis to pass one another abreast without danger to paint; if the resplendent woodwork of doors and window sashes was left to blister in the sun and grow streaky with rain-carried grime; if the entrance halls were stripped of their carpets and the rooms of the furniture and in place of these were substituted the crazy household goods of the worse than poor; if the rooms were inhabited by a whole family — and sometimes more than one; if the stairs were broken and holes gaped in walls and roofing so that on wet days every wall showed blotches of grey; if the passages and stairs and rooms and roadway were filled with shrieking, whooping children in every stage of uncleanliness, then you would have Lower Water Lane, which winds its way crookedly to the Creek bridge and eventually to Greenwich.

There are certain forms of architecture, however, just as there are certain types of humanity from which the pristine beauty cannot ever be wholly effaced, and the houses of Lower Water Lane, in spite of the mud and grime and slime that engulfed them, still maintained a shadow of their faded dignity.

Mr. Evelyn, the diarist, walked once along the narrow pavement, and watched the leather-breeched workmen fitting the lead gutterings. Peter the Great working in the dockyard nearby, got drunk regularly at the inn at the corner. Poverty began to trickle into Water Lane in the late forties when the gentry moved up to Blackheath and, rat-like, burrowed itself into cellars and basements and could not be ousted, gradually creeping up until it reached the attics, where it stole the lead gutterings, while a lower stratum removed all superfluous panelling and cupboard doors and used the wood to light its fires.

The police down Lower Water Lane walked in twos and carried their truncheons conveniently up their sleeves. Sometimes a big police car would dart into that squalid thoroughfare, disgorging the Flying Squad from headquarters, and there would follow a wailing and yelling from some dark interior, the sob of a woman bereft of her husband, and the car would go silently away amid the execrations of the neighbours, carrying an extra passenger.

Into this noisome alley, where every conceivable crime known to the mind of man was bred and flourished, came Dr. Hartley — a very different Dr. Hartley to the well-groomed man who had left Scotland Yard barely an hour previously. A visit to Harley Street had resulted in a considerable change in his appearance. A three days' stubble of beard concealed the smooth firmness of his chin, and his clear grey eyes had become red-rimmed and bloodshot.

His pallid cheeks sunken and grimed

with dirt were in direct contrast to the brick red of his nose which had curiously lost its shape and become thick and bulbous. His boots were a travesty, split and gaping, and the fringes of his dilapidated trousers were not long enough to conceal the inch of bare flesh between them and the tops of his boots. A dingy muffler partly covered the grey shirt, and with the collar of his greasy jacket turned up about his ears and a ragged cloth cap pulled down over his eyes he shuffled down Lower Water Lane towards the Pewter Pot.

A cold, dank river mist filled the narrow thoroughfare with feathery wisps, rendering it difficult to see more than a few yards ahead, and from the river came the dismal wailing of ships' sirens and the mournful hoot of a tug as the traffic on London's waterway cautiously felt its way down stream.

Hartley limped along, covering the ground with that quick-stepping gait that was part and parcel of his disguise — a shadowy figure among the many shadowy figures who brushed by him, intent on their own business or pleasure, without so much as a glance.

He was two-thirds of the way down the lane when he saw his objective, or, rather he saw the blurred lights of the bar reflected on the mist, and presently reaching the swing-doors he pushed them open and entered. There was no class distinction about the Pewter Pot. There were no saloon bars and public bars. There was one bar, and one bar only — a big, bare, frowsy place, with sanded floor, and lit by incandescent gaslights enclosed in big white globes, on which generation after generation of flies had left their marks.

A few tables and rickety chairs for the convenience of customers, several coloured prints of dubious subjects completed the furnishings. Across one end of the low-ceilinged room stretched a long bar, presided over by the owner of this sink of iniquity — the Slogger. He was best described as an enormous man — enormous in girth and height, enormous in face, and hands, enormous in strength. A veritable giant, with large, outstanding ears, low receding forehead, and little black, beady eyes like currants in an overbaked pudding that were set so close to his broad nose that they were almost lost behind the bridge.

He was smartly, almost over dressed, and in his flaming tie and on his dirty fingers diamonds glittered in the lights above the bar, while across his capacious waistcoat gleamed a cable of gold watch chain.

An impressive figure, thought Hartley, as he slouched over to the bar and ordered a rum from the shirt-sleeved potman — a man whom one would think twice about before tackling. His drink was banged down in front of him, and he paid for it out of a handful of greasy coppers. When he had gulped down half the fiery spirit, he took out a cheap packet of cigarettes, lit one, and looked about him.

The bar was crowded with a heterogeneous collection of humanity.

★ ★ ★

There were Germans, Frenchmen, Dutchmen a sprinkling of many nationalities, and their raucous chatter filled the room with an unmusical din. The Pewter Pot had never been built for a public-house. It had originally been a mission-hall, had been converted from that to a storehouse, and, after a long period of emptiness, had finally been purchased by the Slogger and put to its present use.

Hartley had expected a low joint, but the squalor which he saw around him was worse than he had anticipated. The place was so filthy that it amazed him that any human being would put up with it. The only visible attempt at cleanliness was the sand on the floor, and this had been put down with such a sparing hand that it might just as well never have been put there at all.

He finished the remainder of his drink and ordered another. When it arrived and he had paid for it, he slouched over to a vacant table by the bar which he had noticed and sat down.

Nobody took any notice of him, and from this point of observation he began to take stock of his surroundings, never moving his head, but only his eyes, and keeping the cloth cap pulled down well over his forehead.

One thing struck him immediately and that was the uncomfortable, unfriendly air of suspicion about the place. All the frequenters seemed to be divided up into little groups, and it appeared to the watching doctor that all of the groups seemed to be antagonistic, and were watching each other covertly.

Sipping his drink and puffing at his cigarette, he waited keenly vigilant and with straining ears for any sign or chance word that would help him in his search for Henry Arthur Young, alias Silverton. It was ten chances to one, of course, that he was wasting his time — the precious time that was so short — but there was nothing else for it. This was the only place where he could hope for any clue at all, and he reasoned that there was a strong possibility that, since Young or Silverton was such a close friend of the Slogger, he would get in touch with him.

The minutes slipped by, however, and nothing happened — not a word or an action to give him the line he sought

— and Hartley began to feel a sense of helplessness. It wanted but a few minutes to closing time — indeed the potman was already shouting 'Time, please!' — and the doctor was on the point of giving it up and going when the door was pushed open roughly and a man entered.

He was a little, wizened, sharp-faced individual, dressed in a mackintosh obviously too big for him, and, without glancing to right or left, he shouldered his way through the various groups and made for the bar. The Slogger had evidently been expecting him, for the moment he caught sight of him he signalled for him to come up to the other end of the bar, which was practically deserted. The little man gave a quick, bird-like nod and went over. With a glance round him, he leaned across the bar and began whispering to the proprietor.

Without much hope that he would learn anything, but determined to miss no opportunity of doing so, Dr. Hartley rose from his table, which was but a few paces away from them, and, approaching the bar, banged on it with his glass to attract the potman's attention. The Slogger looked round sharply as he did so, but, apparently coming to the conclusion that the disreputable relic of humanity was harmless, went on with his low, rapid conversation.

'Rum,' growled Hartley hoarsely as the potman came over.

'Yer only just in time, mate,' grinned the man, and took his glass to the back of the bar.

While he was measuring out the spirit, the doctor strained his ears to catch the conversation that was going on between the Slogger and his companion, but all he could hear was a low hum. It was not until he was turning disappointedly away with his drink that he caught two words, but they were sufficient to cause a little thrill of excitement to flash through him.

'Tell Harry — '

The rest of the sentence was lost as the Slogger lowered his voice, but Hartley stiffened at the name.

'Tell Harry!'

Could the Harry referred to be Henry Arthur Young? Probably not. There were thousands of Harrys. On the other hand, perhaps. At any rate it could do no harm if he kept an eye on the wizened man.

The customers of the Pewter Pot were beginning to drift out, in twos and threes. The little man finished his remarks to the Slogger and laid a pound-note on the bar. The proprietor nodded his large head, and, going to a cupboard at the back, took out a bottle of whisky, which he wrapped in a sheet of newspaper and handed to the wizened man, who stuffed it into the pocket of his mackintosh. There was a further whispering, and then the little man scooped up the change which the Slogger put down beside him, grunted a 'Good night,' and hurried out of the building.

As quickly as he dared, Hartley gulped down his rum, wiped his mouth on the back of his hand, and shuffled out after him. The mist had given place to a drizzling rain, and he saw the wizened man walking rapidly down the lane, and caught a momentary glimpse of his mackintosh as he passed under the sickly light of a lamp-post.

Dr. Hartley set off in pursuit. It might be a wild goose chase; on the other hand it might not. In any case, it was all there was left for him to do. So far, his efforts had been without result. His quarry proceeded without a pause looking to neither right nor left, and presently plunged down a side alley. On, on he went, twisting and turning through dark, evil-smelling passages, until at last he came out by the river. The tang of tar and cordage reached the doctor's nostrils and the lap, lap of the water mingled with the patter of the rain. The bulk of moored vessels, their twinkling mast-lights gleaming against the black of the sky, made blots of darkness to his right. The man he was following kept steadily on, and came at last to a rotting wharf. Going to the end of this he paused, looked down into the water, and then began to climb down what must have been a ladder, but was invisible to Hartley.

The doctor waited until he had disappeared from view, and then, he too cautiously made his way to the end of the wharf, and lying flat, so that he couldn't be seen, peered over the edge. The little, wizened man had got into a boat, and was in the act of casting off.

Hartley's pulses beat a trifle faster. Had he found a line to Silverton after all? It certainly looked like it. The man was obviously not a waterman, and if he had been merely in search of a bottle of whisky, there were at least half a dozen public-houses nearer than the Pewter Pot.

Hartley was in a quandary. There was no other boat near at hand, and by the time he had found one he would lose his man. There was only one thing to do — he would have to swim for it! Making his way down the ladder, he let himself slip gently into the water. It was icy cold, but he clenched his teeth and, guided by the faint creak of the rowlocks, struck out in his quarry's wake.

15

On the Barge

The pitch blackness of the night made Hartley's task of following the boat containing the wizened little man anything but an easy one, for he had to rely almost entirely on his sense of hearing.

The man appeared to be keeping to the left bank of the river, hugging the moored vessels that reared their hulls out of the lapping water and became lost in the shadows. Hartley swam with powerful, silent strokes and presently caught a glimpse of his quarry as the rowing-boat moved farther out and became for an instant silhouetted against a patch of light that flickered an uneasy reflection in the water.

The boat went on downstream, the rhythmic plash of the oars plainly audible above the distant river noises.

Dr. Hartley followed, praying fervently

that the man wasn't going far. Already he was numbed with the cold and the weight of his clothes rendered swimming difficult. A tug hooted somewhere behind him, and presently went past too close to be pleasant, its wash breaking over his head. He blinked the water out of his eyes and peered ahead for his quarry. There was no sound of oars, and for a second Hartley thought that he had lost him, then dimly he made out the shadowy blot of the boat. The occupant had stopped rowing, and was evidently waiting for the tug's wash to die down. Hartley trod water and waited, too. After a minute or two the river became calm again, the little rowing-boat stopped bobbing about like a cork, and the wizened man once more bent to his oars.

But this time he headed for mid-stream and it soon became clear to the doctor that he was making for the opposite bank. With the inward hope that no more traffic would pass, at least until he was out of the way, Hartley altered his course. It had been comparatively easy with the tide, but it was a very different matter now.

By the time he had reached the middle of the river, Hartley became aware that there were treacherous cross-currents. It was as though some hidden monster with many tentacles was pulling at his legs and his arms ached and his whole body cried out in sympathy with them when he eventually succeeded in crossing the broad waterway. The boat with his quarry had pulled in under the shadow of a barge that lay moored to a buoy, and hanging on to the slimy pile of a wharf, panting and nearly exhausted, Hartley watched the wizened man secure it to a trailing rope and swarm up another on to the deck.

In spite of his physical discomfort, the doctor felt a thrill of excitement tingle his pulses. Was his bow, drawn at a venture, going to hit the target, after all? Was his visit to the Pewter Pot, made on the almost hopeless off-chance of picking up a clue, going to bear fruit? It certainly looked like it. There must be some very real reason for this man to have gone so far just for the sake of buying a bottle of whisky. Of course, the whole business might have nothing whatever to do with Henry Arthur Young, alias Silverton. There were plenty of Harry's, and an intrigue of one sort or another was the habitual atmosphere of Lower Water Lane and its surrounding district, but that sixth sense that occasionally came to the doctor whispered that he was right — that somewhere on that barge was the man he was looking for.

He waited until he had recovered from his battle with the river currents, and then swam slowly in the direction of the dark bulk of the barge into whose shadows the man in the mackintosh had vanished. He reached it, and grasping the gunwale of the rowing-boat, pulled himself aboard and began to massage his cramped and numbed limbs. In a little while he had restored the circulation and started to consider his next move.

Obviously the first thing to do was to make sure that he hadn't come on a false errand — that Silverton was really somewhere on the barge. To do that it was essential that he should explore it, and so cautiously and without noise he began to climb up the dangling rope hand over hand.

This was an easier proceeding than he had imagined, for he discovered that it had been knotted at regular intervals, and a few seconds later he found himself standing on the deck. Looking round, he saw that there was a low cabin amidships from the side of which a dull gleam of light shone.

On tiptoe, cursing the flop-flop of his sodden shoes, Dr. Hartley made his way over to this dim splash of radiance. It came from an oblong window almost flush with the deck, and stretching himself full length the doctor peered in through the dirty glass. At first he could make out very little, for the heat from inside had coated the pane with moisture, but presently he was able to see dimly a table over which swung an oil-lamp.

On the table stood the bottle of whisky, and sitting facing him was the little wizened man who had brought it from the Pewter Pot. He was talking to another man seated opposite him, but to the doctor's chagrin, he could only see this second person's back. Was it Silverton. As if in answer to his question the man rose and crossing the tiny cabin, opened a cupboard built into the wall.

As he returned to the table carrying two glasses, the light from the hanging lamp shone full on his face, and with a pang of acute disappointment Hartley realised that the man was a stranger. He was a stout, red-faced, clean-shaven man, as utterly unlike Silverton as it was possible to imagine. All Hartley's hopes fell to the ground like a house of cards. His evening had been a waste of time after all.

Well, it would have been an almost unheard of piece of luck if it had turned out otherwise, but this philosophical thought didn't compensate for the feeling of failure. What could he do now? A clock somewhere on the shore jerkily tolled out the hour. Midnight! Twenty-four hours only remained for him to find the Black Idol, and he hadn't the faintest idea where to start. However, the first move was to get off this infernal barge and go back to Harley Street and get out of his wet clothes.

He moved with the intention of rising to his feet and as he scrambled to his knees a hand gripped him by the collar and jerked him roughly to his feet.

'Now then!' grated a harsh voice. 'What the blazes do you think you're doing, there, eh?'

And at the sound of that voice Dr. Hartley received the biggest surprise of his life. It was Silverton!

'Come on, answer!' snarled his captor, shaking him violently. 'Who the deuce are you, and what are you doing spying about this barge?'

Hartley thought rapidly. His disguise was a good one. Would it deceive the keen eyes of the man who was holding him? He decided to try, at any rate. Letting his muscles go limp, he allowed himself to hang flabbily in the other's grasp.

'I ain't doin' nuthin',' he whined with a pronounced Cockney accent. 'Reely I ain't! Let me go, guv'nor!'

'How did you get on board this barge?' demanded Silverton suspiciously.

'Fell inter the river,' answered Hartley, searching his brain for a feasible story. 'Was lookin' for some place ter doss, an' fell off a wharf in the dark.'

Silverton's grasp on his collar relaxed.

'Well,' he grunted, 'you'd better fall into the river again. We don't want you here.'

He gave the doctor a push that sent him staggering back against the cabin.

Silverton's voice had evidently reached to the ears of the two men inside, for the door opened and a stream of light cut a wedge into the darkness.

'What's all the row about?' asked the little wizened man, mounting the short flight of steps that led up to the deck. 'What the deuce did you want ter go out for? Are you mad, with the busies — '

'Hold your tongue, Brin!' snarled Silverton. 'I found a fellow spying into the cabin.'

The man in the mackintosh uttered an exclamation.

'Who is he?' he asked sharply.

'Here he is,' answered Silverton, catching Hartley by the arm and swinging

177

him round into the light. 'Says he fell into the river while he was looking for somewhere to sleep. Best thing is to throw him back — '

'Throw him back nothing!' cried Brin, peering at Hartley intently. 'There's something fishy about this feller. He was at the bar of the Pewter Pot when I was buying the whisky.'

Dr. Hartley's heart sank. For a moment he had thought his bluff was going to succeed.

'At the Pewter Pot, was he?' said Silverton. 'That's a long way from here — a long way to come looking for a doss.'

'I was told there was a plice down — ' began Hartley, but the other stopped him.

'You shut up,' he snapped roughly. 'We won't take any risks, Brin. Take him down into the cabin and we can talk over what we're going to do with him.'

Hartley set his teeth. Once in the lighted cabin, and it would be all up. His immersion in the river must have played havoc with his make-up. It was good enough to have passed muster in the dark, but in the light it was a different matter. There was only one thing to do — make a dash for it.

Suddenly wrenching his arm free from Silverton's hand, the doctor clenched his fist and lashed out. The blow caught the other full on the chest and he staggered backwards. Before he could recover, Hartley had swung round and made a spring for the side. The little wizened man was, however, quicker than he was. Like a streak of lightning he reached the doctor's side and bending down, gripped him by the knees. Jerked off his balance, Hartley crashed to the deck, and the next moment was rolling over and over fighting desperately to free himself from the clutching hold of Brin. He had partially succeeded when the third man took a hand.

Standing over the struggling combatants, he waited his opportunity and then planted a well-timed kick in Hartley's ribs. The savage assault drove every vestige of breath out of the doctor's body, and he collapsed as limp as a pricked balloon. Before he had a chance to recover, Brin had scrambled to his feet, and with the help of the red-faced man picked Hartley up, carried him down the steps, and flung him on the floor of the cabin.

'Now,' growled Silverton, shutting and barring the door, 'I'd like to hear all about you, my beauty!'

The doctor's cap had fallen off during the fight, and, coming over, Silverton uttered an oath.

'By cripes! Dr. Hartley!' he muttered.

But Dr. Hartley scarcely heard him. His eyes were fixed on a squat object that stood in one corner, its malignant face seeming to sneer with an evil smile as it caught the light.

His quest had ended sooner than he had expected. He had found the Black Idol!

16

A Chance of Escape

Jill Marsh woke from a fitful doze and discovered that during her sleep somebody had entered the silk-hung room and left a covered tray on one of the low inlaid tables. The sight of it made her realise rather to her surprise that she was ravenously hungry. She lifted the spotless napkin and found a plate of cold chicken, a salad, some bread-and-butter and half a bottle of Burgundy.

She finished the meal and felt considerably better. The tall Chinaman evidently had no intention of starving her. She wondered if the letter he had forced her to write had reached its destination, and tried to picture Jack's consternation at its contents. Of one thing she was certain — if the Black Idol was in his possession she was as good as free, provided her captor kept his word. Provided he kept

181

his word! She repeated the sentence mentally, and a vague doubt began to creep into her mind. Would he? Once the thing he wanted was in his possession would he keep his promise and let her go? Wouldn't it be far more likely that for his own safety's sake he would take every precaution to ensure that she couldn't lay information with his description before the police? She tried to put the thought away from her, but it kept on recurring insidiously until she was more than half sure that she was right. It would be so easy. No one knew where she was and once she had served their purpose what was to stop them from — She shivered at the picture her imagination conjured up. There was nothing to stop them. The more she thought of it the more depressed she became, and was unaware that this state of mind was more than half due to the reaction of the drug that had been administered to her.

Supposing it was their intention to make away with her directly they got possession of the idol, what could she do to prevent it? Nothing! She was completely in their power, and utterly helpless. She didn't know even what time it was, or whether it was day or night. She rose in a sudden panic and began to pace the room. Presently the physical movement began to calm her mental state, and she racked her brain for some means of escape. If only she could get away — get out of this horrid room with its embroidered hangings and its faint, nauseating perfume!

She came back to the table and drank the remainder of the Burgundy, and, sitting down rested her chin in the cup of her hand, and thought hard. Since there was a way into the room, there must be a way out. The tall Chinaman had made his exit with the letter behind the hangings on the right wall. If she could find that exit — She went over, and, pulling back the silken draperies, began to examine the panelling carefully.

The door or sliding panel, or whatever it was, was somewhere about the centre. She had noted that much, and there must be some means of opening it from this side as well as from the other. She ran her fingers up and down the beading in the hope of finding some projection; but there was none, and all her pressing on the panels themselves yielded no result. The wall appeared entirely solid. Jill was on the point of giving it up in despair when she heard the faint shuffle of footsteps.

They came from the other side of the wall, and were gradually getting louder as the person who approached drew nearer. Someone was coming! A brilliant idea flashed to her brain. If she only had some sort of weapon. — She looked about her quickly, and her glance fell on the empty Burgundy bottle.

In three noiseless steps she was at the table, and in three more was back again, crouching by the hangings grasping the neck of the bottle firmly in her right hand. The approaching footsteps had stopped and with her heart beating so wildly that she was certain it could be heard by the person outside she waited tensely. There was a soft click as a bolt was withdrawn, and then a gentle sliding sound. The hangings were pushed aside, and a short, squat figure shuffled through the opening. It was a little Chinaman.

He was dressed in a short blue jacket, and he peered forward with extended head. As he saw the apparently empty room, a faint sibilant hiss left his lips, and he was in the act of turning his face in Jill's direction when the girl sprang forward and brought the bottle down with all her strength on the back of his unprotected head! The blow was a heavy one, for the bottle broke in her hand, but it had the desired effect. Without a sound the Chinaman staggered, and collapsing on to the thick carpet, lay still.

For a second the girl felt the room spin about her, but with a strong effort of will she mastered her momentary faintness and stepped hurriedly to the hangings. The Chinaman had let them drop behind him, but when she pulled them aside she saw with a feeling of relief a narrow oblong gap in the panelling.

Almost holding her breath, she slipped through and found herself in a richly-carpeted corridor that led apparently to a broad landing. Pausing, she listened intently, but the stillness was profound, — there was not a sound anywhere — and after a second or two to recover herself she began to creep forward towards a dim light that shone from somewhere below, and which, she concluded, was the hall of the house.

She reached the landing, and found that on her right was a wide staircase that led downwards. It was lit by a big orange-shaded lamp that hung from the ceiling and ended in a square vestibule luxuriously furnished. Evidently she was in a house of some size. What was her next move? Obviously she couldn't stay long where she was. Several doors opened off the corridor she had just traversed, and at any moment someone might come out of one of these and discover her. Equally obvious to descend that staircase was risky. At the same time, it couldn't be long before the Chinaman in the room in which she had been imprisoned recovered consciousness and gave the alarm, and in that event all chance of her escaping would be gone. She decided to risk the staircase.

With her heart thumping in her throat, and her ears strained for the slightest sound, she crept down stair by stair. She succeeded in reaching the hall without mishap. Directly in front of her was a massive door, evidently the main door of the house. She tiptoed towards it, and was halfway across the polished parquet when the sound of someone approaching brought her to a sudden stop. The footsteps came from the back of the house, and were drawing rapidly nearer. Jill looked hastily about her, searching for somewhere she could hide, but the hall offered not a scrap of cover.

There was only one thing to do. She must take a risk and trust to luck. Opening off the hall were two doors to right and left, and both were closed. She chose the left-hand one, and prayed that it might be unlocked and that the room beyond would be empty. The person who was approaching was getting unpleasantly near when she turned the handle softly and pushed.

The door opened to her unbounded delight, and she slipped into the darkness of the room beyond. Closing the door, she waited breathlessly her hand clutching the handle. She heard somebody cross and go into the room on the right. For what seemed an eternity there was the tinkle of glass against glass, and then the footsteps passed by outside again. She listened as they retreated and faded to silence, and then cautiously emerged, peering round the half-open door to assure herself that the hall was deserted. She discovered that it was, and continued her interrupted journey to the big door. It was bolted and the chain was up and with infinite care she drew the heavy bolt from its socket and unhooked the chain.

A second later she was opening the massive door inch by inch. It was evidently night for outside it was pitch dark, and she heard the patter of falling rain. Squeezing through the partly-opened door, she saw a flight of steps leading on to a gravelled drive, and that was all she had time to see, for at that instant she heard a shrill cry behind her.

A wave of terror swept over her, and leaping down the steps, she began to run frantically along the sodden gravel. The thud-thud of pursuing feet reached her ears above the drumming of her heart, and panic lent her speed. She flew along the dark drive, her breath coming in great panting gasps. It took a sudden turn to the right, and as she rounded the bend she ran full tilt into someone who was coming in the opposite direction. She heard a guttural grunt, followed by a sibilant exclamation and hands grasped her arms.

With an access of strength of which she would never have believed herself capable, she wrenched herself free and continued her headlong flight. There was a muttering of voices behind her, and she doubled her speed. A sharp pain was stabbing at her side, and flashes of red floated before her eyes. She felt as if her feet were shod with lead, and twice she stumbled and nearly fell. An opening appeared before her — a pale patch against the blackness — and she saw the bleary reflection of a lamp on a strip of shining pavement and then the patch was blotted out as a second figure loomed in her path! She tried to dodge past it, but failed, and felt her arm gripped.

'Let me go!' she panted. 'Let me go!'

But the grip on her arm tightened.

'Good heavens, Jill!' cried a voice and with a thrill of thankfullness she recognised it as belonging to Jack Mallory, before everything went black, and she collapsed fainting in his arms!

17

Jack Takes a Hand

Dr. Hartley and Eric had hardly left Mallory Hall for London when Jack began to wish fervently that he had gone with them. In an excess of restlessness, he prowled about the house, walking into one room and out again, drifting disconsolately about the passages like a lost soul, a prey alternately to the blackest depression and the brightest optimism.

Four times he strolled into the library where Sir Edward was seated trying to read, fiddled about with things on the mantelpiece and strolled out again. At the fifth repetition of this aimless perambulation, Sir Edward shut his book with an irritable bang, and looked up at his son with a frown.

'For Heaven's sake, Jack,' he snapped angrily, 'make up your mind what you're going to do! If you're going to stop in here, do so; if you're not go somewhere else, but for the love of goodness, don't keep popping in and out. It gets on my nerves!'

'I'm worried,' said Jack apologetically.

'So am I,' retorted his father. 'But that's no reason why I should behave like a blithering idiot. We can't do anything. The matter's in Hartley's hands, and it couldn't be in any better.'

'I wonder what he's doing,' muttered Jack. 'I wish I'd gone with him.'

'I wish you had!' exclaimed Sir Edward with considerable emphasis. 'Either that or gone to bed.'

He picked up his book, and his son, after opening his mouth as though to speak, thought better of it, and walked out into the hall. For a moment he stood looking at the hallstand, and then, apparently making up his mind, he lifted a heavy coat from one of the pegs, and struggled into it. He was just buckling the belt when Rowson appeared.

'Tell my father, if he asks,' said Jack to the grey-haired old butler, 'that I've gone up to London. I'll be back some time tomorrow.'

Rowson bowed.

'Shall I tell Saunders to bring the car round, sir?' he asked.

Jack shook his head.

'No; I'll go and get it myself,' he replied. 'I'm only taking the two-seater. I shan't want Saunders.'

He walked round to the garage, and a few minutes later was driving through the night in his own little sports car *en route* for London. He had no very clear idea of why he was going, or what he was going to do when he got there, but he felt that if he had stayed at Mallory Hall another minute he would have broken something.

He had reached the outskirts of the metropolis before he definitely decided that his first move would be to go to Harley Street, and find out if Dr. Hartley had succeeded in making a move. But here Fate took a hand in his affairs, and it was destined that he should not reach Harley Street after all. The first in the series of events that were to bring about this drastic change in his plans was a sudden and complete stopping of his engine.

It occurred just outside Wimbledon on a stretch of road running along by a patch of common and with an unprintable exclamation Jack got down and raised the bonnet to look for the trouble. Half-an-hour later he was still looking without having attained any satisfactory results. At the end of that time he gave it up in despair and decided to go in search of a garage, get somebody to take charge of his car, and continue his journey to Harley Street by taxi if he could find one.

Leaving the car by the roadside he set off briskly towards a string of lights that indicated civilisation and the possibility of a garage. He had reached a broad, well-lighted street that led downwards to a cluster of shops when the second event happened and completely changed his plans. Coming towards him as he walked rapidly along he saw the tall figure of a man. He was moving quickly, and they passed each other almost under a street lamp.

Jack glanced casually at the other from

under his cap as he went by and nearly stopped dead in his surprise. It was the tall Chinaman from whom he had taken the Black Idol at Moat Farm! In the sudden shock of amazement Jack nearly gave himself away, and it was only by a supreme effort that he forced himself to continue on his way. The Chinaman had not recognised him — of that he was certain — and Jack made up his mind to follow him. Crossing the road, he swung round and went back on the other side.

A hundred yards ahead the Chinaman was still walking along at a sharp pace, and evidently completely unconscious that he was being followed. Jack kept him in sight, his heart beating rapidly with elation. It was an extraordinary piece of luck to have run into the man like this. It mattered very little now whether Hartley succeeded in finding the Black Idol or not. The man who had so audaciously abducted Jill would lead Jack to where the girl was kept prisoner, and he could communicate with the doctor at once.

The tall Chinaman turned down a wide road to the right, and, keeping judiciously in the rear, Jack followed. Big houses, standing in their own grounds, flanked the thoroughfare on either side, and about two-thirds of the way along his quarry turned into the gates of a drive. Jack slowed his pace and hesitated. Should he note the house and telephone Hartley or should he explore further on his own account?

His mind was made up for him. He heard a faint cry in the distance, and then a moment later the sound of running feet on gravel. In order to find out the cause of this disturbance, he crept into the dark entry of the drive and tiptoed forward a few paces. A guttural exclamation in front of him brought him to a halt and then, as a flying figure loomed towards him, he stepped forward and caught it by the arm.

'Let me go!' panted a girl's voice, and Jack realised who it was he was holding.

'Good heavens! Jill!' he exclaimed, and caught her as she fell limply into his arms. Before he could make any further move he felt himself roughly seized and the girl was torn from his arms. He swung round. Three shadowy figures launched themselves upon him from out of the darkness clinging to him like leeches. Jack got in one blow, and a little stunted man fell with a high-pitched screech, but after that he found himself helpless. Hands of incredible strength seized his arms and held them prisoned to his sides. Somebody caught his ankles, and despite his frantic struggles he felt himself hoisted up and carried. He opened his mouth to yell for help in the hope that some chance passer would hear, but his attempt was frustrated at its birth. Something was crammed into his mouth and held there, and he found it difficult enough to breathe, much less anything else.

He was carried along until presently he saw the bulk of a large house loom up in front of him. An orange light streamed dimly from an open doorway. There was a chattering of shrill, excited voices in Chinese and then an order was rapped out authoritatively in vibrant sibilants.

Jack was taken up the broad steps and on a wide staircase. He heard the thud of a closing door, was borne rapidly along a dark corridor and flung down on to a couch of some description. Before he could move busy fingers were at work at his wrists and ankles, and in a few seconds he was bound and helpless.

A light sprang to life, and looking about him he saw that he was in a small, barely-furnished room that resembled a servant's bedroom. He was lying on a narrow bed and the only other furniture consisted of a washstand and a chest of drawers. Four little yellow-faced men in ill-fitting clothes were grouped by the door, watching him with malignant expressions, but at a word from someone outside they cleared away from the doorway, and the tall, thin Chinaman whom Jack followed entered. He came over to the bed and stood impassively looking down at his prisoner. His immobile face set in an inscrutable mask. It was impossible to read the thoughts that were passing in the brain behind that yellow, lifeless mask. For a second he gazed at Jack, his heavy lids drooping over his almond eyes, and he made a gesture with one thin bony hand. The four little Chinamen withdrew noiselessly and closed the door.

Li-Sin stooped and untied the cord which secured the handkerchief that had been thrust into Jack's mouth.

'So,' he said softly, 'once again we meet, Mr. Mallory.' He held up his hand to check the torrent of words that welled up to Jack's lips. 'There's no need for you to attempt to explain. I can guess what you are doing here. You hoped to be able to rescue the white girl and so retain possession of the Sacred Idol.'

'I hoped nothing of the kind,' burst out Jack wrathfully. 'To start with I haven't got your confounded idol. That crook Silverton walked off with it at the Moat Farm after you'd gone. And as to having come here with the intention of rescuing Miss Marsh, that's all nonsense. It was quite by accident that I recognised you in the street a few minutes ago, and followed you.'

'A thief and a liar walk hand-in-hand,' quoted Li-Sin.

'Do you mean you don't believe me?'

roared Jack hotly.

The Chinaman shook his head.

'I do not,' he answered simply. 'You are telling me this story about the Sacred Idol to try and trick me.'

'I assure you — ' began Jack, but the other interrupted him.

'Nothing you can say will make me believe that the Sacred Idol of Tsao-Sun is not in your possession,' he said. 'I have made my ultimatum, and I shall not alter. If the idol is delivered safely to my messenger at the hour and at the place I have already named, both you and the white girl shall go free. If not, then the fate that has been planned for her shall be shared by you.'

He turned abruptly on his heel and in spite of Jack's protestations, left the room without another word.

The key snapped in the lock and his soft footsteps faded to silence.

Jack gazed at the ceiling, cold despair in his heart.

Everything now depended on Dr. Hartley. He prayed fervently that the doctor would be successful, little dreaming that at that moment Dr. Hartley was as helpless as he was himself, and preparing to face an ordeal that had every likelihood of costing him his life!

18

The Victim of the Barge

Silverton glared down into the upturned face of Dr. Hartley, and his lips were curled back in a grin of hate.

'So you have found me have you?' he snarled. 'Well, a lot of good it'll do you. I'll put an end to your spying ways once and for all.'

He drew an automatic from his pocket, and as the ugly black muzzle came to rest in a line with his head, Hartley gave himself up for lost. But the trigger was never pulled. For a moment Silverton hesitated waveringly and then, still keeping the gun aimed at the doctor, he turned to Brin and the other man.

'Get some rope and tie him up,' he ordered. 'We'll finish him in some other way. This is too noisy. Somebody might hear the report.'

Brin nodded and disappeared up the

steps leading to the deck. He returned very shortly with some lengths of tarred rope, and with the assistance of the other man secured Hartley's ankles. Crossing his hands behind him, they bound those too, and then tied them to the rope about his legs.

'He'll be clever if he can wriggle out of that,' grunted Brin, when he had finished surveying his handiwork with satisfaction. 'What are you going to do with him?'

'I'll discuss that presently,' answered Silverton. 'In the meanwhile gag him, and then as soon as Wally turns up we can get to business.'

He watched while Hartley was skilfully gagged with a lump of cotton waste that reeked of oil and had apparently been used for cleaning the swinging lamp and then, going over to the table, he searched in a drawer, found a corkscrew and opened the bottle of whisky.

Pouring out three stiff drinks, he gulped down his own, refilled his glass, and lighted a cigarette.

'Did you ask Slogger to have the boys in readiness in case we should want them?' he asked.

'Yes,' answered Brin, smacking his lips with relish after a long drink of the neat spirit. 'He's going to pass the word round.'

'Then if Wally's in time we can get the whole thing settled before dawn,' said Silverton. 'You've got your gun?'

Brin patted his hip pocket and nodded.

'And you, too, Marks?'

'Sure, boss,' replied the other man with a grin.

They went on smoking and drinking, and taking no more notice of Hartley than if he had been a log of wood. What was it that was going to be settled before dawn, thought the doctor. Evidently something that depended on the arrival of the unknown Wally and necessitated the use of guns. Were they contemplating a raid on a bank or some similar premises? Silverton's next words helped to enlighten him.

'Wally ought to have been a detective,' he remarked. 'He's the cleverest fellow for nosing out things I've ever met. Now if he's really found out where this Chinese fellow lives, we'll go and force him to show us how the blooming idol opens, get the jewels, and clear out of the country.'

'If there are any jewels,' grunted Marks, pessimistically.

'I'm sure there are,' asserted Silverton. 'I've verified the legend. I'm not so sure about the explosive in which they are supposed to have been packed, but the jewels are there right enough.'

'Well, if there's any way of opening that thing,' said Brin with a glance at the Black Idol, 'I'll eat coke. It seems ter me as solid as a house.'

'All the same,' answered Silverton, 'there is a way, and this Chinaman knows it. That professor fellow knew it, too. It's all set down in manuscripts which he got hold of, and that's why he was killed.'

'It's going to be pretty risky, boss,' put in Marks, 'attacking these guys. They're nasty fellers ter deal with.'

'I know that,' said Silverton. 'Haven't I had some? I've got a score to settle with that tall, thin brute for burning my foot — the hound. But I don't care how risky it is. I've done the big to get hold of those jewels, and I'm not going to have all my trouble for nothing.' He looked at his watch. 'It's time Wally was here by now.'

He poured himself out another drink and pushed the bottle across the table.

So that was it, thought Hartley, listening. Wally, the absent one, had discovered where Li-Sin was to be found, and Silverton, accompanied by a gang of roughs got together by the Slogger, was planning to force him to disclose the secret of the idol. Knowing something of Chinese cunning and resource, the doctor wondered who would come out best. He was inclined to think that Silverton had bitten off more than he could chew. However, the main thing that occupied his mind at the moment was how he could get free.

He had already made furtive experiments with a view to loosening his bonds without result. Brin was evidently an expert, for, try as he would, Hartley couldn't move the fraction of an inch. Something had to be done, for the doctor had no delusions regarding his ultimate fate. He could expect no mercy from

Silverton. The man was desperate, and what was worse, a born killer. He knew that if he was caught the Death House loomed in front of him. It was a hanging matter, anyway, therefore another murder wouldn't make any difference. Dr. Hartley racked his brain to think of some plan, but his imagination failed him utterly. Bound as he was, he was helpless, and he hadn't the least idea what was in store for him — what Silverton intended doing with him.

He was still vainly endeavouring to formulate a scheme when there came a footfall on the deck, and presently the thud of booted feet coming down the steps. Somebody tapped a peculiar knock on the door of the little cabin, and Brin went over and unlocked it. A tall man in a tightly-fitting dark overcoat and soft felt had entered.

'Hallo, Wally,' greeted Silverton. 'Well, what's the address?'

'High Hill House,' answered the new-comer shortly. 'Just off Beech Avenue, Wimbledon. Is that whisky you've got there?'

Silverton chuckled.

'It is,' he grinned. 'The Slogger's best. Help yourself — you deserve it.'

Wally, whose appearance suggested that of a respectable city clerk, helped himself in silence, and then, as he set down his empty glass, he caught sight of Hartley and started.

'Who's the boy friend?' he asked.

'Oh, let me introduce you,' said Silverton with a sneer. 'The greatest Nosey Parker of modern times, Dr. James Hartley!'

'Dr. Hartley!' Wally breathed. 'What's he doing here?'

'Poking his nose into things that don't concern him, as usual,' replied Silverton. 'This time I'm afraid he's got to get it pulled badly.'

'What are you going to do with him?' said the man called Wally quickly.

'Make certain that he doesn't interfere in any affairs again,' was the reply.

'You mean croak him?' asked the other.

Silverton nodded.

'You're very quick on the uptake, Wally,' he said easily. 'That is exactly my meaning, and while I attend to Hartley you and Marks had better go over to the Slogger's and round up the boys. He's got together six of them — with us, that makes ten. There'll be two taxis waiting near the 'Pot.' You take the first and get along with Marks and the other three to this place, High Hill; I'll come along in the other after I've finished here.'

'Right you are.' Wally poured out another whisky, gulped it down, and beckoned to Marks. 'Come along,' he said. 'Where do I meet you, Harry?'

'At High Hill,' answered Silverton. 'What is it like — the house — a big place?'

'Fairly,' said Wally.

'Standing in its own grounds?'

'Yes.'

'Got a drive?'

'Yes.'

'Then wait for me just inside the drive,' ordered Silverton, 'and tell the boys — your lot — to keep well hidden until I arrive with the rest.'

'All right!' Wally nodded quickly. 'So long.'

'So long,' said Silverton, and when they had gone came over and looked down at Hartley.

'I'm afraid,' he said softly, 'that your career is about to terminate, Hartley. In a few minutes I shall be leaving this barge for good. The idol, of course, will go with me, but I regret that I shall be compelled to leave you behind.' He paused and his lips curled in an evil smile. 'As I shall have no more use either for you or this barge, you might as well both go together.'

A vague idea as to his meaning flashed to the doctor's brain, but Brin looked puzzled.

'What yer going ter do?' he asked doubtfully. 'Yer ain't going ter leave 'im 'ere alive, are yer?'

'I shall leave him here alive,' replied Silverton, 'but I can assure he won't be alive very long after. It is practically high tide, or will be in a few minutes. Just before we go we shall remove the bilge plugs. It should take about half an hour for this old tub to fill, and when it finally settles in the mud at the bottom of the

210

river this stateroom will contain a passenger!'

'I see,' said Brin. 'Yer goin' ter sink the barge and drown 'im?'

'Crudely put,' said Silverton, 'but that is the idea. Now let's hurry.'

He went over to the cupboard and brought back some sacking with which he wrapped up the Black Idol.

'Here you are,' he said lifting it and giving it to Brin. 'You take this to the boat and wait for me. I'll join you in a second or two.'

The little wizened man departed with a nod, carrying the sack-covered idol, and Dr. Hartley watched Silverton drain the remainder of the whisky with cold despair in his heart. There was not one chance in a million of his escaping. Bound hand and foot and unable to move he would be drowned like a rat in a trap — dead long before the old barge finally vanished for good beneath the swirling waters of the river. It was a horrible death, and in spite of his iron nerve, the doctor felt a shiver run through him.

Setting down his glass, Silverton went

over to the door. On the threshold he paused and looked back.

'Goodbye, Hartley,' he said. 'I hope you have a comfortable journey!'

With a harsh laugh, he went out, and Hartley heard the key click in the lock. For a long time there was silence, and then faintly to his ears came the sound of gurgling water. Silverton had removed the plugs! A footstep thudded on the deck, followed after a pause by the creaking of oars, and then silence once more. From somewhere in the distance came the faint hoot of a siren. The swinging lamp flickered, turned blue for a moment or two, flared up with a last spurt of energy, and went out, leaving Dr. Hartley to face the rising of the water in darkness!

19

The Attack on High Hill

Henry Arthur Young, alias Silverton, was not by any stretch of the imagination a great criminal. He was as far removed from the master-crook beloved of fiction writers as a butcher is from a Harley Street surgeon. But he was possessed of a ruthless nature that stuck at nothing to gain its own ends, and an obduracy and tenacity of purpose that, put to better use, might have got him anywhere.

It was this very obstinacy that had caused him to make up his mind to wrest the secret from the Black Idol at all costs. From the moment that he heard Jack Mallory discussing the image with Dr. Hartley in the smoking-room of the homeward bound liner, and learned the story of the hidden jewels, he came to the conclusion that here was an easy way to the wealth that his twisted soul craved.

That it had not been so easy had rather upset his calculations, but never for one moment had he thought of giving the whole thing up as a bad job. Even at the Moat Farm, when things appeared to have reached a climax, his quick brain had found a way out, and not only a way of escape but a way by which he was enabled to re-possess himself of the Black Idol when he thought he had lost it for ever.

And now, as, accompanied by Brin, he made his way towards the Pewter Pot, he felt full of elation that the successful conclusion to his planning and scheming was within sight. He suffered from no qualms of conscience regarding the terrible fate which he had left Dr. Hartley to face on the derelict barge. Rather was his feeling one of satisfaction that he had been able to penetrate the doctor's disguise, and so be enabled to take precautions against the danger of arrest, which had been very near.

If, after being cooped up in the little cabin all day, he had not decided to take a breath of air on the river and returned in time to catch Hartley spying about the deck, he would probably have been in a cell by now instead of free, with a quite respectable chance of getting clean away with a fortune.

It had been pure luck. Well, he hoped that his luck would hold. The most dangerous part of the business still lay ahead of him, and yet he couldn't see, with care, how it could go wrong. There would be ten of them all armed, and taken by surprise, the inhabitants of High Hill should be easily overcome. Silverton had promised the 'boys' as he called them — a collection of roughs from Lower Water Lane, who would have been capable of killing their own flesh and blood for a fiver — a substantial reward for the night's work.

By the time he and Brin, still carrying the sack-swathed idol, arrived at the Pewter Pot, the first taxi containing Wally, Marks and three of the others had departed for Wimbledon. The Slogger met them at the back entrance, and in answer to Silverton's question nodded his huge head.

'Yes, Harry,' he whispered, 'they're waiting for you just along by Wharf Alley. You'd better hurry up. I shouldn't keep Wally and the first bunch hanging about too long in case somebody from the house gets wind of what's going on. If you can take them by surprise, you've won half the battle.'

Silverton agreed.

'I'll be off at once,' he said. 'So long. I'll come back here after for a minute or two.'

'All right, Harry.' The Slogger gripped his hand with a grip that made Silverton wince. 'Good luck!'

They came out of the narrow passage that led round to the back of the Pewter Pot and turned to the left. A few yards along the road the red light of a tail lamp glowed dimly. Silverton approached the waiting taxi and opened the door. Two roughly-dressed men who were seated inside, made room for Brin, and after a word to the muffled driver Silverton got in and they drove away.

During the journey he discussed his plans, which were of the simplest. They would meet the others at the end of the drive, make their way cautiously to the house, where the rest of them would take up positions each side of the front door. Silverton himself would knock. Directly the door was opened they would emerge and force their way in, holding up the inmates at the point of their pistols. It all sounded beautifully easy and free from risk. The two gangsters hired for the purpose declared that it was a 'blinkin' walk-over.'

They made good speed through the silent, deserted streets of the City, and in less than an hour from leaving Lower Water Lane, drew up a few yards beyond the wide entrance that Jack Mallory had entered earlier that night.

Silverton glanced quickly about as he got out of the taxi, but there was not a soul in sight. Marshalling his men hurriedly, he made his way towards the drive. Farther along the road he saw the dim lights of a car drawn up by the kerb, and concluded rightly that it was the taxi in which Wally and the others had arrived.

The night was dark, but the rain had

ceased, and except for a dank clamminess in the air, it was fine. Entering the drive, he paused in the pitch darkness and whistled a low minor cadence. An answering whistle from close at hand assured him that the others were at their posts.

'Is that you, Harry?' a voice whispered almost at his elbow, and a figure loomed out of the blackness.

'Yes,' murmured Silverton. 'Everything O.K., Wally?'

Wally replied in the affirmative.

'Then come on, let's get it over,' said Silverton.

He briefly outlined his scheme, and like phantoms they crept up the broad, winding drive. Their rubber-shod feet made no sound on the strip of grass that bordered the gravel, and presently they rounded the bend and came in sight of the house. It was in darkness — not a ray of light gleamed from any of its windows, and the fanlight over the door was like a sightless eye.

Silverton gave a grunt of satisfaction.

'Everybody's in bed,' he whispered. 'All

right, take up your positions each side of the door.'

He mounted the steps, the others following, all except Brin, who was still carrying the Black Idol. On each side of the front door was a wide recess, and in these they crouched, their pistols held ready in their hands.

Drawing his own automatic, Silverton raised his hand, and, grasping the knocker, beat a thunderous tattoo on the door. He heard the sound echo through the silent house and waited. A minute passed, and then, a light sprang to life in the fanlight and a shuffling step approached the door. There was a rasping of drawn bolts and the clank of a chain and then the heavy door swung back, disclosing the shrunken figure of a little yellow-faced Chinaman silhouetted against the light.

Before he could open his mouth, Silverton sprang forward, and, gripping him by the collar of his loose blouse, rammed the muzzle of his pistol into his skinny neck.

'Make a sound and I'll send you to blazes,' hissed Silverton.

The little Chinaman's eyes opened wide and his mouth gaped, but he kept silent.

'Come on in and shut and fasten the door,' whispered Silverton, and the waiting gangsters came noiselessly into the hall.

The door swung to and the bolts were slipped home.

'Now,' went on Silverton, 'bind and gag this guy, one of you, while we find how many more there are in the house. It's the tall, thin fellow, Li-Sin, that I want a word with. You can do what you like with the rest.'

Leaving the little yellow man trussed up like a chicken in the hall with one of their number mounting guard over him, the rest explored the house. Five other Chinamen were discovered sleeping in various bedrooms, and, taken by complete surprise, were treated in the same way as the first. It was Silverton who found Jack, and for a moment he was puzzled, then he recognised the young man.

'So they got you did they?' he

220

muttered. 'Well you're better where you are and the best thing is to leave you there.'

He continued his search for the tall Chinaman, and although he twice passed along the corridor outside the room in which Jill Marsh was concealed he had no idea of its existence or even that the girl was in the house, for the sliding panel had been well constructed and even had he been looking for it would have defied detection. The raid had been so swift and silent, that scarcely a sound had broken the stillness after that first knock on the door.

Silverton explored the second floor without result, but as he was descending to the first landing he met Wally.

'He's in there,' he whispered and pointed to a door on the right.

Silverton's eyes narrowed and, gripping his automatic more firmly, he noiselessly opened the door and peered in. A soft light burning from a silver wall lamp cast a dim radiance over the luxurious bedroom, and lying on the bed, a narrow divan-like affair of rich silks, was Li-Sin!

His head rested on an embroidered pillow and he was asleep.

Silverton crept across and bending down placed the cold muzzle of his pistol against the sleeper's head.

At the touch of the steel the Chinaman opened his eyes, caught sight of the menacing figure of the crook above him and started up with a guttural cry.

'Good evening,' breathed Silverton softly, but with a vicious snarl lurking at the back of his silky tones. 'This is a pleasant surprise. I don't suppose you expected to see me again.'

After the first start of surprise the Chinaman regained his normal impassive expression. His eyelids drooped and he surveyed Silverton through the oblique slits imperturbably.

'What is it you want of me?' he asked so softly as to be almost inaudible.

'I'll tell you what I want,' hissed Silverton harshly. 'Get up, and don't try any tricks or I'll put a stream of lead through your ugly yellow head!'

In silence Li-Sin looked at him, and then rising, slipped his arms into a thickly-padded, heavy silk dressing-gown.

'Put on some more light,' ordered Silverton, and Wally, who had remained by the door, pressed down a silver switch near the lintel. A large shaded cluster in the centre of the ceiling glowed into rainbow hues.

'That's better,' Silverton nodded. 'Now,' he went on to the tall motionless figure by the divan, 'we won't waste any more time. I want to get away from here as soon as possible. All I want you to do is to tell me how to open that idol.'

Li-Sin gave an almost imperceptible twitch to his eyebrows.

'So,' he murmured, 'that is what you want of me.'

'That's what I want,' agreed Silverton, 'and that's what I'm going to have, so you'd better come across with the information quickly and save a lot of time — and trouble,' he added significantly.

'So,' said Li-Sin again, 'then the Englishman Mallory was speaking the truth when he told me that the Sacred Idol was in your possession.'

'He was,' answered Silverton. 'Very

much so. In fact I've got it here with me now. Come on, tell me how it can be opened and look sharp.'

The other shook his head slowly.

'I shall never tell you that,' he replied with dignity.

'Oh, won't you!' Silverton's eyes snapped angrily. 'We'll see about that! Call the boys,' he ordered, without turning his head, and Wally slipped from the room. 'You were kind enough when last we met,' continued Silverton, the words dropping from his thin lips like slivers of ice, 'to try a little experiment on me with the aid of a lighted candle. I have not forgotten it — you yellow scum!' For a second his eyes wavered towards the fireplace. 'I propose to try an elaborated edition of that experiment on you.'

'Whatever you do, you can never make me speak,' declared the Chinaman, drawing himself up to his full height. 'I would sooner die than divulge the secrets entrusted to me by the priests of the Temple of Tsao-Sun.'

'It won't be a question of dying,' snarled Silverton. 'Dying would be easy compared to what I intend to do to you if you don't tell me what I want to know.'

Li-Sin said nothing, only his thin lips curved in a slight smile.

Wally returned accompanied by four of the slouching roughs whom Silverton had collected to help him in his expedition.

'Lay him on that couch thing and hold him down,' directed Silverton, and when his order had been obeyed, 'Now bare his chest.'

'What yer going to do, guv'nor?' asked one of the gangsters as this instruction was carried out.

'You'll see in a moment,' said Silverton with a chuckle, and going over to the fireplace stooped down to the object on which his eyes had momentarily rested a few seconds before. 'Give me a hand here, Wally.'

Wally came over with a rather puzzled expression.

'What's the idea?' he demanded. 'What are you going to do with that thing?'

'Make him talk,' snapped Silverton, and picked up the portable electric radiator. 'Look after that flex, Wally. I think there's enough to reach.'

The radiator was a square affair of oxydised silver, its open front covered by spirals of twisted wire. Silverton carried it over and laid it on the Chinaman's bare chest, so that the wire coils rested in contact with the flesh.

'Now,' he said triumphantly, 'there's no need for me to tell you how this thing works. When the current is switched on these spirals of wire become white-hot! The sensation, I should imagine, will be anything but pleasant, but you must admit it's a distinct improvement on the candle — about a thousand candle-power improvement.' He laughed and laid his hand on the switch at the side of the radiator. 'I'll give you until I count three,' he said, 'and if you haven't agreed by then to tell me how the idol opens, I'll switch on the current!'

The almond eyes of Li-Sin gazed up at him calmly.

'One!' said Silverton.

Dead silence, not a flicker of the drooping lids or any hint of expression on the immobile yellow face.

'Two!'

A faint contraction of the muscles and a slight compression of the thin lips — nothing more.

'Three!' said Silverton, and pressed the switch!

20

The River Thieves

Dr. Hartley lay staring into the darkness concentrating every atom of his intelligence in trying to evolve some means of escaping from his terrible predicament. Struggle and twist as he might Brin's knots remained firm, and at last he gave it up, his wrists sore and chafed, and his muscles aching from the strain of his cramped position.

How long had he got before the end? At the moment there was no sign of the water that he could hear gushing through the bilge plugs, but it couldn't be long before it entered the cabin and slowly rose inch by inch. It wouldn't require so many inches either before his interest in the fate of the barge was over. The way he had been tied up had rendered movement impossible. He had tried repeatedly to raise himself into a sitting posture, hoping by that means to put off the seemingly inevitable by a few minutes, but soon discovered that this was physically impossible.

Breathless from his exertions, he relaxed for a second and suddenly felt a cold clammy touch stealing beneath his body! Rolling on to his back he found that the floor was wet to his fingers. The water had already entered the cabin. At that rate it would be less than fifteen minutes before it rose high enough to cover his mouth and nostrils, and then —

Hartley gave a little shiver. Death was very near, and there seemed no hope. His mind went to Eric. He would like to have had a last word with the boy. What would happen to Jill Marsh now? He had failed lamentably, but he had done his best. One couldn't do more than that. Still, he would rather have gone out in a fair fight, with at least a sporting chance. To die like this, caged up and drowned like so much vermin, was horrible.

His thoughts flitted from one subject to another. Little odd, half-forgotten incidents in his life rose to his mind unbidden, unconnected pictures that had no beginning and no end. Over-strain must have brought on some kind of delirium, for he experienced a sudden blank, and when once more he returned to a full realisation of his surroundings the water was lapping his chin. Well, it wouldn't last much longer now, and the sooner it was over the better. It seemed ages since he had felt the first trickle on the floor — a whole lifetime. He had to keep his mouth closed and breathe through his nostrils. Another minute at the most.

Dr. Hartley resisted a supreme effort to hasten the end and let himself sink beneath the cold soft water, but almost in spite of himself his subconscious mind cried out to him to ward off death until the last possible moment. With a considerable amount of trouble and no little pain, he managed to twist himself on to his knees and knelt precariously, swaying backwards and forwards. It was doubtful if he could retain that position for long.

His hands bound to his ankles forced

him to bend his body back in a bow, and it was difficult to keep his balance, but it would give him a short respite.

His spine was a searing agony, and his head throbbed madly. Splashes of vivid white and orange stabbed the blackness before his burning eyes. His senses were swimming and he thought almost with relief of the peace and rest beneath that cool water, and then suddenly he heard a sound, and the shock of it restored his mental alertness.

It was the murmur of voices, and the sound of stealthy footsteps on the deck above. For a moment Hartley thought that he was suffering from an hallucination, but the voices grew louder and the feet began to descend the ladder leading to the cabin. A moment later the latch was rattled vigorously.

'The door's locked,' grunted a rough voice. 'May be somethin' worth 'avin in 'ere.'

'Let's bust it open,' replied another voice almost identically like the first. 'We'll 'ave ter look slippy, though. This old tub must 'ave sprung a leak by the look of things.'

Dr. Hartley felt his heart leap with hope. At the eleventh hour it seemed that help had arrived, and from a totally unexpected quarter.

There came a tremendous thud on the door, followed by another, and then with a splintering crash it gave way.

The light from an electric torch spreading fan-wise wavered through the darkness and came to rest on Hartley's head raised a foot above the water.

A sudden loud exclamation from the owner of the torch told the doctor that he had been seen.

'Cripes, Joe!' cried the first voice in amazement. 'There's a bloke's 'ead 'ere stickin' out of the water.'

'What yer talkin' abaht?' growled Joe, and then, as he waded into the cabin: 'By Gosh, so there is! An' 'e's bin gagged, too. Come on, there's somethin' fishy 'ere, Bob. Let's see what's up.'

They advanced and the man with the torch tore the gag from Hartley's mouth while his companion held him up.

'What's the matter, mate?' demanded Bob. 'Who did this on yer?'

The doctor was too. exhausted with the strain of his ordeal to answer.

'Undo my wrists and ankles,' he gasped.

They lifted him on to the table, and with a clasp knife produced by Joe from some unaccountable pocket in his ragged clothes, slashed through his bonds. While Hartley was rubbing his numbed wrists, he took stock of his rescuers. They were typical river rats of the kind that haunt the docks and wharves on the chance of picking up a living by stealing stray bits of cargo during the unloading of a ship or of making off with anything loose that may be lying about a boat that has been left unguarded. It was purely providential that they should have chosen to turn their attention to the barge and arrived in the nick of time.

Seeing that they were about to question him again, Hartley decided to pitch a yarn that was in keeping with his appearance. He told them that he had been asked to do a 'job for a feller,' that he had met the 'feller' by appointment on the barge, and the 'feller' had tried to get out of paying. There had been a row and two other chaps who had been with the 'feller' had tied him up, and left him after pulling out the bilge plugs.

The two river thieves swallowed the story, although they evinced a decided curiosity concerning the 'feller's' identity and the nature of the 'job' that Hartley had done. Hartley, however, fell back on the cunning of the kind he was impersonating and eventually, after making sure that there was nothing worth taking from the cabin, they rowed him ashore in a dilapidated boat, which apparently they had 'borrowed' for the occasion, and left him.

Dr. Hartley was shivering with the cold caused by immersion, but he had no time to go home to Harley Street and change. There was still a chance that if he hurried he would be able to catch Silverton before he left High Hill, and his first objective was a taxi. There was very little likelihood of finding one in the vicinity of Lower Water Lane, and to keep himself warm he ran all the way to Deptford Broadway, where he eventually succeeded in finding a cab. The driver looked at him suspiciously, until he gave his destination, but even the most suspicious taximan couldn't find anything wrong with Scotland Yard.

At the grim building on the Embankment, Hartley found Gladwin, and briefly told his story. Two minutes after his arrival wires were buzzing with orders, and ten minutes after that two long, fast police-cars left the entrance for High Hill, packed with men from the Flying Squad. Hartley had succeeded in borrowing a warm overcoat from his friend, Inspector Gladwin, and this helped to take the chill from his wet clothes, though he felt far from comfortable, and sat in a clammy atmosphere that rendered the journey unpleasant to say the least of it.

The first thing that Hartley noticed as they drew to a halt by the entrance to High Hill, was the two taxis standing up the road by the kerb. A quick examination by one of the plain-clothes men with him, showed him that they were empty and the doctor's eyes narrowed. They were in time.

Followed by the Scotland Yard men, Hartley and the sergeant-in-charge made their way up the drive.

'You'd better station men at all possible exits,' suggested Hartley as they came in sight of the house, 'and then if you and the rest wait by the front door, I'll see if I can get in somewhere at the back, and open it for you. I warn you, however, that we shall be dealing with a desperate man in Silverton.'

'All my men are armed, sir,' said the sergeant, 'though I hope it won't come to a shooting scrap.'

'I share your hope,' answered Hartley grimly, 'but I'm afraid it will. Silverton will hang if he's caught and he knows it, so unless we can take him unawares he's going to show fight.'

'Perhaps it would be better if we waited until they come out,' suggested the sergeant, 'then we could take them by surprise.'

'Except for one thing,' said Hartley, 'that would undoubtedly be the best plan, but I've reason to believe that Silverton is trying to force some information from the

Chinaman who owns this house, and I wouldn't like to say to what lengths he'll go to try and get it.'

'You mean torture?' asked the horrified sergeant.

Hartley nodded.

'Then there's only one thing to do, sir,' declared the Yard man. 'We shall have to break in somehow and risk the consequences.'

They had arrived at the house by now, and the doctor saw that the hall was lighted, and that a light also shone from one of the upstairs windows. Even as he looked two shadowy figures crossed the drawn curtains — big, shapeless, blurred blotches.

'Station your men, sergeant,' he whispered, 'and then wait at the front door. If I don't let you in in ten minutes you'll know that I've been caught and you'd better break your way in.'

'All right, sir,' said the sergeant, and with a nod Hartley left him and made his way round to the back.

There were no lights here of any description, and he explored until he found a ground-floor window that was latched, but unlike the others, had not been shuttered. Hartley searched about, and presently found what he wanted — a heavy, fairly large stone from a strip of rockery that edged the path. Wrapping it in his sodden muffler, he tapped sharply on the window-pane.

The glass splintered with a tinkling crash, and, inserting his hand the doctor pressed back the catch and raised the sash. The next instant he had swung his legs over the sill and was standing within the dark and silent house. As his eyes became accustomed to the darkness, he found that he was in a small room that was obviously used as a store. Several boxes and packing-cases stood against the walls, and opposite the window was a partly-opened door.

Inspector Gladwin had lent him an automatic, and gripping this in his hand, Dr. Hartley stole over to the door and slipped through. It opened into a passage, and by the dim orange light that shone at the end the doctor was certain that the passage led to the hall.

He listened, but there was no sound, and, tiptoeing down the narrow corridor, Hartley ascended three steps, and found, as he had expected, that he was in the vestibule. Crossing the wide expanse of polished parquet he cautiously raised his hand and pulled back the bolts of the front door. He was in the act of undoing the chain when there came a hoarse shout behind him and swinging round, he found himself looking into the muzzle of a pistol held in the grimy hand of a short, roughly-dressed man who was leering at him from the shadow of the big staircase.

'Now then, you!' rasped a voice menacingly. 'You leave that chain alone and put your hands up — quick!'

21

The Last of the Idol

Dr. Hartley slowly raised his hands keeping his eyes fixed warily on the man with the automatic, and then, when they were almost above his head, he dropped suddenly to the floor. There was a whip-like crack, and a bullet thudded into the door above his head. Hartley's own automatic spurted flame in reply and the man by the staircase gave a yell of pain and, dropping his pistol, clutched at his wrist.

Hartley was on his feet like lightning, and almost in one movement had jerked the chain off its hook and pulled open the door. The sergeant followed by half a dozen plain-clothes men, streamed into the hall.

'This way!' said Hartley as he heard a chorus of excited shouts from upstairs and led the way up the staircase.

A door on the first landing was open and a stream of light poured out. The doctor caught sight of a group of figures huddled together on the threshold, and as a fusillade of shots whistled round his head he charged among them, scattering them right and left. One glance he took of the interior of the room and its occupants and his face set grimly. On a silk-covered divan lay the figure of Li-Sin. His face was white, or as near white as his complexion would allow, and wet with perspiration, and he was unconscious. On his bare chest rested a square object which Hartley recognised as an electric radiator. Bending over the figure on the divan, his lips drawn back in a snarl of fury, was Silverton, and by his side stood Brin and Wally. On a small table at the foot of the divan was the Black Idol! The air was heavy with the smell of scorching flesh . . .

Dr. Hartley took in these details in one quick glance, and then, covering the three with his automatic, he stepped sidewise and backed against the wall.

'The game's up, Silverton!' he cried

coldly, although his blood was boiling at the savage cruelty that had been enacted in that room. 'Take that thing off his chest and put up your hands!'

But with dropped jaw Silverton was staring at the man he had believed dead.

'Dr. Hartley!' he muttered hoarsely. 'How in heaven's name did you get here?'

'Never mind how I got here!' snapped the doctor. 'Take that infernal thing off now, or I'll drop you!'

Silverton obeyed like one in a dream, and Hartley winced as he saw the terrible burns that crossed the bare flesh.

'You deserve horsewhipping, all of you, for that act of devilry!' he said through his teeth.

'I had nothing to do with it,' whined Brin. 'He was in the middle of it when he called me up with the idol. I didn't — '

'Hold your tongue!' rapped Hartley.

Pandemonium was going on outside. The crack-crack of automatics mingled with bloodcurdling curses and shrill cries of pain, and then suddenly through the open doorway staggered a plain-clothes man and one of the gangsters locked grimly together fighting desperately. Right into the line of fire from Hartley's automatic they came and Silverton seized his opportunity. With a snarling cry of hatred he leapt forward and before the doctor realised his intention had snapped down the light switches. The light went out, plunging the room into darkness.

Hartley made a bound for the door and gripped an arm. Somebody kicked out at him and caught him an agonising blow on the shin. He lashed out with his right, and heard a grunt as his bunched fist landed on flesh. An arm was flung round his neck from behind, and he fell crashing to the floor with steel-like fingers digging into the flesh of his throat. His unknown assailant rolled over on top of him, and the pressure on his windpipe increased.

Hartley let himself go limp, and then suddenly shot up his knees, with all his force. The grip on his throat relaxed as his opponent shot over his head and landed with a thud that shook the room. Hartley staggered to his feet, and as he did so a vicious tongue of flame spat out almost under his nose.

It was impossible to go on fighting in the dark unable to tell friend from foe. Crouching down to avoid the danger of a chance bullet, Hartley felt his way to the door and searched for the light switches. He found them at length, and flooded the room with light.

Such a picture of wild disorder he had seldom seen. Two of the plain-clothes men were lying on the floor still and lifeless. In one corner crouched an unshaven gangster nursing a leg from which the blood streamed copiously. Brin was struggling in the grip of a Yard man, who, even as Hartley looked, brought the butt of his pistol down on the crook's head and put an end to the fight. Li-Sin was sitting dazedly on the edge of the divan, evidently just recovered from his faint; but of Silverton there was no sign, nor was the Black Idol still on the table. The table had been overturned and was lying with its legs smashed against the wall, but the idol had vanished.

There was still a furious uproar going on outside, and Hartley and the plain-clothes man who had knocked out Brin went out into the passage to see what was going on.

The light from the door illumined it dimly, and one glance showed the doctor that the police were getting the upper hand.

'It's all right, sir,' panted the breathless and dishevelled sergeant. 'I think we've got the better of them now.'

'Have you got Silverton?' demanded Hartley, and even as he asked the question realised that the sergeant didn't know Silverton from Adam.

'I don't know, sir. Is he among this lot?' asked the man indicating the battered roughs that were held in the grasp of his equally battered men.

'No,' snapped the doctor, and hurried to the head of the stairs. He was just in time to see Silverton crossing the hall holding in his arms the Black Idol. 'Stop!' shouted Hartley, and then, before he could move a figure rushed by and went flying down the stairs. It was Li-Sin! He was within a foot of Silverton when the crook turned with a snarl and raised the idol above his head. His intention was to bring it down on the Chinaman's head, but it was never realised. One of the plain-clothes men, seeing what was about to happen, levelled his automatic and fired. He had aimed at one of Silverton's arms, but the shot went wide and struck the Black Idol full in the centre of its ugly body. There was a flash of blinding white flame and a deafening explosion that shook the whole building. A great wave of wind rushed up the staircase and sent Dr. Hartley staggering backwards, and the hall became filled with a dense cloud of black smoke.

When it cleared away there was nothing of the idol or the two men who had been there a moment before — nothing but a great mound of debris from a ragged hole in the roof and a cloud of dust that was wafted about in the draught from the shattered front door.

★   ★   ★

'So far as the explosive was concerned,' remarked Dr. Hartley, 'the legend was certainly true. If there were ever any jewels, they must be blown to dust by now.'

He was seated in the consulting-room at Harley Street, drinking the steaming hot coffee that Wilson, the doctor's man, aroused from sleep, had grumblingly prepared.

Jack Mallory and Jill Marsh were sitting side by side on the deep settee, and though they both looked drawn and haggard, there was no mistaking their cheerfulness.

'I personally don't care whether there are any jewels or not,' said Jack. 'I'm jolly glad the idol's gone for good, and can't do any more damage.'

'Who was the poor beggar of a Chinaman, guv'nor?' asked Eric. 'It seems a shame that he should meet a death like that. After all, he was only trying to get back the idol for the people to whom it belonged.'

'That poor beggar of a Chinaman as you call him,' said Dr. Hartley gravely, 'was Li-Sin, Prince of the House of Tu Lin, of Tsao Sun.

Eric whistled.

'All the same, he was a poor beggar to suffer a fate like that,' he said.

'Every man's fate is tied about his neck,' quoted the doctor. 'And now I think as it's long past dawn, and I've had nothing to eat for over twenty-four hours we'll get Wilson to cook us some breakfast after which — '

Dr. Hartley turned to Jack and Jill — 'I'm going to bed, and Eric will drive you two to Hailsham.'

'Via the nearest registrar's office,' said Eric, as he noticed that the girl's hand was clasped in Jack's. But he said it to himself, so nobody heard him.

THE END

We do hope that you have enjoyed reading this large print book.

Did you know that all of our titles are available for purchase?

We publish a wide range of high quality large print books including:
Romances, Mysteries, Classics
General Fiction
Non Fiction and Westerns

Special interest titles available in large print are:
The Little Oxford Dictionary
Music Book, Song Book
Hymn Book, Service Book

Also available from us courtesy of Oxford University Press:
Young Readers' Dictionary
(large print edition)
Young Readers' Thesaurus
(large print edition)

For further information or a free brochure, please contact us at:
Ulverscroft Large Print Books Ltd.,
The Green, Bradgate Road, Anstey,
Leicester, LE7 7FU, England.
Tel: (00 44) **0116 236 4325**
Fax: (00 44) **0116 234 0205**

Other titles in the
Linford Mystery Library:

DEATH ASKS THE QUESTION

John Russell Fearn

Seemingly grand from the outside, the interior of Abner Hilton's house was a dilapidated, gloomy place — reflecting its morbid and desperately impoverished occupant. But Hilton's insane plan would lift him out of his poverty. He would murder his young niece, who was about to visit him; her dead father's will would ensure that her considerable wealth would pass to him. However, when his plan was put into operation, the young woman's horrifying death was to have terrifying repercussions . . .